Liminal Island

Sithethile Sgwentu

Published by Sithethile Sgwentu, 2024.

LIMINAL ISLAND

First edition. May 12, 2024.

ISBN: 979-8224816859

Written by Sithethile Sgwentu.

Liminal Island

<u>Keith</u>

When I'm rich I want one of those big houses with a balcony and a room for every activity. I want a mattress and full bottles of hand soap in each bathroom. I want one of those electric fans and a big silver fridge. My fridge will be filled to the brim, practically rotting with only the best food. I want to be disgustingly rich. Most importantly, when I'm rich I won't have to deal with idiots like Mr Rain.

Mr Rain was this guy Mickey and I worked for. We delivered food across the rich side of the island and at the end of the month we got paid. That day, there happened to be early signs of a glass storm. Mickey didn't want to work but I told him we would be fine. We needed the money anyway.

Of course it was January, a particularly broke month for everybody. I get why Mr Rain cheated us out of a pay check. I just wished he coulda been smarter about it. You know how dumb you have to be for Mickey to realize? He says, like he's the new Einstein: "Well you guys do take some of the supplies home and if you add those costs it amounts to your pay check." Mr Rain was a scary looking guy. Real tall. I started chewing on the skin around my fingers. I could feel Mickey thinking about a smart ass thing to say. "Ok Sir, we understand. Thanks." I turned and walked. Mickey followed because we were already drenched in rain and there was no use arguing when you're sopping wet.

On the way home Mickey muttered something about letting the adults talk. He was twenty one so technically he was an adult. I didn't think of him that way, I guess it's because we had known each other forever. Besides I was seventeen, that was adult enough. I stopped doing school when I was fourteen and I've been working ever since. It's not too bad, I got more time on my hands that way.

Lanky is the guy I live with ever since my parents dipped. He's kinda older, a real good guy. Unlike most of us over on the poor side he had a wooden house instead of a shack. I mean, he only had a wood house because it was his grandmas. He used the back of the house for the bootlegged alcohol store he and Mickey ran. It wasn't a massive cash generator but it was enough to get us by.

Anyway Mickey dropped me off at home and rushed to get Lotus from work. Lanky had just finished up in the store. "Hey kiddo, how was work?" I didn't need to tell him nothing. Instead I smiled and told him it was fine. What's the use of causing trouble?

Lanky fixed us some peanut butter and jam sandwiches for dinner. "I've got some things to do in the store, ok? Call me if you need." I listened to his footsteps fade, the loud clank of the metal gate and the jingle of bootlegged bottles. I reached underneath the couch and lit a cigarette. Before I could even put the damn thing in my mouth, Mickey and Lotus walked through the door. Lotus was this chick Mickey was serious about. She was real nice, had a job on the rich side and everything. She sat down next to me and messed with my hair. "I heard about work." she whispered so Mickey couldn't hear. I nodded my head. Mickey mumbled something about "beating the living daylights" out of Mr Rain. Of course he heard us, those ears could hear anything. "Oh, ja?" I stood up with the cigarette in my mouth. I held an imaginary gun, pointed it at Mickey. I closed my left eye and leaned to the side. "What for, Mickey Mouse?" I took aim, looking directly at his forehead.

"Jesus kid. I'm trying to help you here. Come on! Let's teach him a lesson, beat him black and blue. That's the only way to get through."

"Oh so you're a poet now, huh? With all your goddamn rhymes." I pulled the trigger and made a loud bang sound. Mickey put his hand on his forehead and then looked at me with horror, he dropped down to his knees and gasped. He reached his hand out to Lotus.

"You got me Keith...you got me. Oh Lo, please help me!" Lotus simply ignored both of us and walked down the corridor to Lanky's bedroom. We were always messing around like that, she was used to it at that point. Mickey and I were still on the ground, he pressed his rubber heel into my forehead.

"Lo, what are you doing in Lank's room?"

"Giving him a love letter of course." Mickey didn't like jokes like that. Lotus, who knew that, explained that Lanky got a stack of letters from the mail.

"I'm just putting them in his room, no need to stress....Mickey Mouse."

<u>Lanky</u>

I think I was losing my mind. Everything was always so full, I was so busy all the goddamn time. We had so many things that needed fixing. The store was making some money, when you split it up between Mickey and I it was a bit of a joke. I mean, it was enough for Keith and I to get by and his job also helped but ja. We bought a new fridge last August. Which reminded me, that we needed to fill it. It was practically empty, Keith was losing weight and I didn't know if that was my fault or if it was because he was getting taller. God, being old is the worst. Not to mention Keith never spent time with me anymore because I don't know, he was out partying or whatever. I guess I was the boring dad. Which was fine, as long as he was ok, It just made me realise how lonely I was.

Mickey managed to find himself a really nice girl. She came by sometimes on the weekdays while I was at the store. She would quietly sit behind the counter and eat her lunch. She was a real sweet girl, she even tried to set me up with one of her friends, well she tried multiple times.

Here's an example for one of her attempts:

"Hey Lanky."

"Yeah?"

"There's this girl that I work with, she's really cool. Her name's Amy, she's here for a gap year before university. I think you'd like her. I could se-"

I interrupted her. "Gap year? Lotus, my angel I can't date an eighteen year old. Jesus, that's only one year older than Keith."
Keith is not my son, obviously. It would have been a bit concerning if I had a son that old. His mom, well she's like my grandaunt's kid's half-sister or something. It's really terrible what happened to his parents . Nobody ever talks about it, Keith pretends like they abandoned him. It's much easier and less gory than reality. So, when he was thirteen I ended up with him. It's weird being a dad now, it puts things on hold. I didn't have a good dad so I'm not sure how to do this whole thing. I guess parents get a lot of pressure to make sure that their kid isn't a screw-up.
Don't get me wrong, I really am grateful for Keith. It's natural for people to fall off the wagon from time to time, but he's always been a good kid. A little saint he was, and even now after everything, there's nothing I would change about him. I wouldn't change a thing.
<u>Odette</u>
I had only been on the island for a couple of days and it already felt like home. Mama and Tata insisted on moving to a new place every time a hint of boredom arose. When I was a little girl we lived in Paris until I was five. From age five to ten I lived in Botswana and from age ten to sixteen I lived in South Africa. Of course, we travel any opportunity we get. But Tata and Mama said we would be staying on the island until I finished my schooling. I was being home-schooled since there were no proper schools on that remote little island. Tata even bought a little private beach just for us. The house we were staying in was fine, a small little two story with an open plan kitchen.
Alex was my new friend there, she lived with her father who was an acclaimed art dealer. She was from England and had been on the island for a couple of months when I met her. We were both new to the place but she knew her way around a lot more than I did. The island was split into two parts, the rich side and the poor side. There's a long mountain that breaks the two sides. It has a massive man-made hole in the middle

called "The Mountain Pass". It seemed a little rude to dub one place as more well off then another but Mama said that's just how people did things there.

Alex came over to tell me about a party that would be happening on the top of the Mountain Pass. "It will be fun, let's go." She insisted. She had this face you could not say no to. We decided that it would be best to not tell Tata and Mama about the party. It wasn't something they would take well. I told them I was invited to Alex's for dinner. "As long as you're around here it's fine." Tata said. I couldn't understand what was on the other side that he feared so much.

The party had already started before we arrived, there were crates of beer and a big bonfire in the middle. Also some bubbling punch concoction. Lots of dancing and off key singing and loud music playing in the background. Of course, when I walked in with Alex everyone was staring at me. I'm used to this, but Alex was a lot more comfortable than I was. She went to grab us two beers and talked
to some of the people on her way. Alex came back with the beers and because I'm polite I took a sip. But only one because unlike Alex, I was not eighteen. Also, beer is extremely high in calories.

Amidst the music and loud talking and beer Alex introduced me to a few people. The sun had set by then and a dark shadow was cast across the whole event. I can't say I remember the names of most of the people we met except for this guy named Mickey and his friend Keith. Mickey was extremely good-looking, almost annoyingly so. People aren't supposed to look the way he did unless you were some famous actor. He looked at Alex and did this half grin, then turned his head to call his friend over. "Keith, come here!" This boy with long black hair and a button nose turned towards us. Light beige freckles were dotted across his cheeks.

"Hi Alex," he mumbled with this almost charming awkwardness.

"Oh hi Keith I haven't seen you in a while, how are things?"

Mickey interrupted Keith, "Tell your rich friends to piss off there's about to be a fight here that they shouldn't see." I thought he was being rather rude.

"What the hell are you talking about?" Keith asked, with genuine confusion on his face.

"I know because I placed a bet, I might not be in the game anymore...but I know the game." Mickey replied, throwing a fake punch at Keith.

"Cheesiest shit I've ever heard." Keith replied, rolling his eyes. He motioned his hand for us to follow him.

"Sorry guys, but you have to leave...apparently."

"That's fine, don't worry about it." Alex was almost blushing at him. She could pass for pretty when she smiled. She was what my mother would call "lost potential." Mickey, walked away, hitting Keith on the back of the head. Keith looked at me and introduced himself. As though he hadn't even noticed me until that moment. This wasn't something I was used to.

"We should probably piss off now," he suggested.

Keith walked us to the Mountain Pass and attempted some small talk, shame he seemed nice enough. I would have taken part in the conversation but I was not very sociable. Him and Alex seemed to be doing ok on their own though. He had dimples when he smiled, he was actually kind of cute. He walked us to the edge of the Mountain Pass. He said goodbye to Alex and squeezed her hand a little.

Then he looked at me and said "Don't be a stranger." While we were leaving Alex whispers so he can't hear. "He's an odd guy don't you think?" I shrugged, "I wasn't paying much attention to him."

<u>Keith</u>

At around nine, Lanky went to his room to sleep. I was about to do the same, even locked up and closed all the windows. Even switched off the vinyl that played 24/7 like background noise. I boiled myself a big pot of water, poured it in a bucket and washed myself in the kitchen. I liked washing myself in the kitchen after dark, when nobody was around. I reckoned that my kitchen was the best place on the whole island. We didn't have a bath tub or anything like that. We were working on it. If there's one thing those rich people don't have, it's a bath in their kitchen.

Once my bath was over, I put the vinyl on. Elton John...yikes. There I was brushing my hair and listening to Elton John on our "couch" which really was a couple empty crates with a blanket over it. My hair was too long. Wavy, stringy black mess that goes a bit past my shoulders. That's when Mickey walked in, absolutely plastered.

"Elton John...the fuck for?" Mickey was a little blunt.

I shrugged my shoulders. "Why aren't you with Lotus?"

"She's babysitting, I would've joined her but apparently I scare little kids. That's not true, right?" Silence. "Damn, well anyway get up. We're going out."

"Nah, go on your own. I wanna sleep."

Mickey stopped and looked at me with his head tilted. His breath already smelled like too much beer. "You look really Asian, man." So many things were wrong with that statement, I swear Mickey was straight out of the 1800s. "Well my mother was Asian, Mouse." He knew that I didn't like to talk about her.

"Yeah, have you ever been to Japan?" Mickey was an asshole when he wanted to be.

"You know I've only ever been here, and she was Chinese." I hate talking about parents. All I wanted was to get my hair dry and sleep.

"Same fuckin thing, both in Europe."

"Are you stoned?"

He laughed and looked at me with his swampy eyes. Insisting on this damn party. No, there was no way in hell I was going to go to that party.

"That chick from the rich side that you were checking out is gonna be there. Alex." By the way, I wasn't "checking her out" that seems creepy. She's cute, that's all. I turned my head to look at him. "Maybe we drop by for five minutes, ok?" Mickey smiled. He was always draggin me everywhere he went.

<u>Lanky</u>

I fell asleep on my bed before I could finish running my errands. I woke up in shivers with drool all over my face and sleep lines on my arms but I still felt exhausted. I needed to let Mickey do more of the work, he barely came to the store in the daytime, never counted how much we made in a day and had the nerve to ask for "leftovers."

I got out of bed and shuffled to the store and took the cash out of the register. Counted it and split it between Mickey and I. Then I made a list of things to get from the Sunday market. Mangos, eggs, milk, hake, two coconuts. I checked the old clock for the time... one thirty in the morning. "Keith!" He was out. So I started making some dough in our brown wooden bowl. The first item that my ex and I bought together. She was so happy when we had some leftover money that Sunday. Went down to the market and got it for thirty rand cheap. I made a simple bread dough and wrapped the bowl in two blankets so it could rise while I went back to bed.

My hair was starting to dread, I needed to cut it soon but whatever. I got a better look at myself in the mirror next to my bed. I didn't usually sleep on my bed anymore, not since she left. I preferred to sleep on the floor. I would take a blanket and lay it on the ground. It didn't get cold there, I didn't mind. I scratched around my drawer for a cigarette and found a stack of letters instead . I never got letters. My heart practically fell out of my mouth when I read who it was addressed to "To Timmy." I tried to open the first envelope, which felt like it had been glued extra strong because my hands couldn't rip it open fast enough. Finally, the letter revealed itself.

Dear Timmy,

I hope that these letters don't get lost in the mail. I know I have not been in touch at all, I'm sorry. It was a really terrible thing to do, to leave you that way. My head was so mixed up that night, I can't even remember what started our fight. I know we said things that shouldn't have been said. You don't understand Timmy, I was so angry I could have said anything and I couldn't care less who I was hurting because I couldn't hear myself.

Well, I couldn't travel as far as I would have liked. I made it to Cape Town of course. I'm now staying in an apartment that I'm renting with a couple of friends. They're very nice people, they helped me find a job. It's a waitressing job at a pub, not much but it's something to get me by. I miss you Timmy. I can see you rolling your eyes as you read over those words but I really do. It would be incredibly selfish of me to say I want you back. All I can say is that I want to see you again. I left my number at the bottom of this page if you could please call me. I understand if you hate me now or if you've moved on. But I would really appreciate being able to hear your voice again.

You know, I've written so many letters for you since I've been here. I never ended up giving them to you but I'd still write them. I figured you might want to read them, obviously I wrote them a while ago. But I think it would be good for you to read them. I packed them in order, so just, think about it ok?

Love, Alice.

Jesus Christ. I was not going to call her. Not after what she had done, she had no right to act like both of us were in the wrong. She was the one who left me and Keith alone. She was the one who left after saying forever. She was the one who called me a "master manipulator" because I try to control everything even though I'm never there. It's not true. She was a liar.

But of course, I find myself ripping up that floorboard and finding that stupid brown box. A stack of little unsent letters in it, all folded twice, carefully lined up. So I open the first one, and I read it because I thought it would be some sort of confession. Her explaining that she was a fucked up person who couldn't deal with commitment. It wasn't me, I wasn't the bad guy.

<u>Alice</u>

Dear Timmy,

I suppose communication was never our strong point, and I should share my feelings with you but I don't know how. So I've decided to write these letters for you to understand what I want to do. Because I know deep down inside you're still mad and confused about what happened that night. So, to explain why I left you in that way I thought I'd explain how things were for me back there, back on the island. Sometime in January, I had made some progress with the house. The kitchen was the only thing that was properly complete, I remember my mother said that the kitchen was the heart of every home. I guess our home must have heart failure. You told me that by your next payday, we would have saved enough for us to buy a couch. Mr and Mrs Dean were planning on selling theirs. We had this extra room upstairs, I would have liked to use it for a little dance room but you suggested a nursery. We were both only 23, that's not old enough for a child. And we didn't have the money for such things anyway, we still don't. Not to mention, you were gone so often cause of work. There for a week, and a week gone for three. Every time you came home we would fight about one thing or another. I felt so trapped in that godforsaken house. "Go out with friends then" I know that's what you would say. I didn't have any friends. I had your friends who tolerated me but much preferred my company when my hand was firmly clasped to yours with my mouth permanently shut except for the occasional fake laugh or pleasant smile. Plus, there wasn't much to do when you were away. So I would go to visit Mom's gravestone. I visited your grandmother's stone as well. I laid fresh roses on all of them but I'm sure the wind has carried them away by now. It's not like you ever took the time to visit them yourself, because you don't like to face things. You don't wish to see things for the way they are. I thought you were a saint trying to protect others, but it turns out you just wanted to protect yourself.

Love, Alice

<u>Keith</u>

That Odette girl was really pretty, she looked like one of those fancy ladies in the old films that played at that one bar. The pretty lady who lived in a mansion and drank wine. I don't know, I guess that's a little weird. But I've always wished I could be one of those cool guys in the old films. I'd have a white mansion, with a football field for a garden. I'd walk around in a suit and read the newspaper or something. Shit, whatever was in that punch was really not sitting right. It got cold as hell in the evening. Felt like the pit of my stomach was warm and everything else was numb. I couldn't tell if it was me or the ground that was tilting sideways.

Mickey came running to me out of nowhere, his floppy hair bouncing up and down as he approached. "Keef, where'd you go?" Dumb question, where did he go? He was the one who dipped ten minutes in. I wanted to ask how the fight went, but his sour mood answered it for me.

"Think the punch at that place was spiked." I groaned, changing the subject. I think I just don't have a high alcohol tolerance. Or at least, I didn't.

Mickey sighed. "Man, don't drink punch at parties. What are you, twelve or something?"

We both started shuffling back to Mickey's house. Lanky would do that thing if he saw me. Where he isn't pissed off but disappointed. It would be easier if he would just hit me like a normal parent. Mickey started mumbling things I was too drunk to hear.

"Man, you know what would be really helpful?" Mickey got like this when he was drunk. He got more stupid than usual.

"What?"

"Learning Kung Fu man, so nobody would fuckin mess with you."

"Right." Constantly entertaining Mickey's bullshit was exhausting.

"I bet you could learn pretty fast, you do kinda look like Bruce Lee."

"Will you quit that already!" I didn't mean for it to come out as a shout, but that ended up being quite helpful because Mickey didn't say anything after.

Leaning around and all, I for sure would pass out in a few minutes. I started thinking about that Alex chick and Odette. Cause that Odette girl was like, probably the most gorgeous human being I had ever seen in my entire life. She was like model pretty, I swear good looking people like Odette and Mickey must come from the same place, although Mickey's like, Italian I thi- "Hey Keef. Let's start a gang." Part of me wondered if Mickey had relapsed.

"Yeah. No." That's about all I could muster. Like I said, I wasn't even in the mood to entertain his bullshit, let alone actually listen to it.

Even so, he went on this manifesto about how there's no way for us to make enough cash or something. About how if we just got four of us to do little jobs we could take what we earn and split it. I told him to drop it. I swear, he's gonna have me arrested one day.

The light mood of our drunk state was punched right out of us when we ran into some kid screeching on the ground. Practically marinated in blood, screaming bloody Mary. I can't stand the look of blood, I immediately threw up all over the place. While I'm dry heaving like a complete idiot, Mickey steps over the kid, about to leave him. But, in a rare moment of humanity he crouched down next to the kid.

"Come here sit up, the screaming is only gonna make it worse." The kid managed to lift his head up a bit and used his forearms to help him level up. He was still laying down, and it looked like rocks or bats were taken to his shins because they were knackered beyond belief. The white shiny bone peeking out underneath the ultra-red flesh. "Yikes, you probably won't be walking anytime soon." Mickey mumbled, which of course made the kid cry even harder.

"These bastards got me, oh it hurts so bad I don't even know what I'm saying." The kid whined, damn his voice hadn't even broken yet, he must have been ten or twelve.

"What bastards?" I asked, wondering if they were still around. I was not about to get into a fight. Mickey, who was clearly thinking the same thought stands up and looks around.

"I don't know their damn names...they're loan sharks. My Dad owes them money." Everybody was using loan sharks back then. Things were just more expensive I guess, nobody had money for nothing anymore. Mickey sighed in disappointment. "Ja well, your Dad should have paid them instead of wasting his money on weed like a complete asshole." Shit I knew this kid! Mickey used to date his older sister.

"Come Keith pick him up and we'll take him home." Mickey ordered, breaking my train of thought.

We carried that kid all the way to his house where we were greeted by his sister. Her and Mickey ended up staying for longer to bandage the kid's leg. I walked myself home because if I had to see more blood I think I would have puked my fuckin oesophagus out or whatever the hell it's called. Unfortunately, not the worst way for a night out with Mickey to end. There could be more ex-girlfriends, and more blood.

<u>Odette</u>

I slipped back in the house through my bedroom, my bed was already made and my clothes freshly pressed. Mama had already been in my room. I was out long after curfew, well aware of the trouble I would get into. I was supposed to be home at half past eight when I went out. I got home at ten. Also, I left a little before six o'clock so I missed my chores. My bedroom was on the other side of the house so I couldn't tell if Mama and Tata were still awake. I tiptoed to my bathroom and quickly washed my face and put on my nightgown. I had been so deep in my own paranoid thoughts that I had not realised that Tata was standing right behind me.

He loomed over me and didn't say a word. I could see in his eyes that he was vacant. There was no use in arguing tonight. He slapped me through the face. "You know what you did, rules are set in place for a reason." The pain left a vibrating sting on the surface of my left cheek. I've learned by now not to hold your face or cry. It would be overreacting, he only hit me once and then it was over.

Of course, the next morning I woke up at five so I could do two hours of cardio since I missed the day before. Mama was up at six to make breakfast. She did not ask where I went or why I was so late in coming home. She only told me to put some ointment on my cheek. "It looks odd." She said. "That purple splotch on your face." I told her that if I hadn't been hit it wouldn't have been there. "No Odette, if you had done the right thing it wouldn't be there."

Tata was a writer so he spent most of the day in his study, Mama would bring him food so most of the day it was just her and I. If I can be completely honest, I don't think they were too concerned with my education. They bought the textbooks and expected me to work through them but that's all.

At the time, I didn't think my mother was a cruel woman, she wanted the best for me. Both my parents wanted me to be a model. Ever since I was little everybody was always telling me that it was the right path for me. Mama managed my diet, exercise and jobs which would hopefully lead me to a successful career in modelling one day. All I had to do was exactly what she says and everything would be fine.

I was interrupted from the television when I heard three knocks on the door. "Mr Rain's Delivery Service!" I sprang up, it felt so strange to have groceries delivered right to our doorstep. Especially since there wasn't a supermarket. One had to wonder how safe the food was. "Coming!" When I opened the door I was surprised to find the guy from the party, Keith. He was holding two wooden crates which were overflowing with food. Mr Rain's Delivery Service could do a better job at packing, I thought. Keith looked flustered as soon as he realised who it was.

"Oh, hey there Odette." He gently placed the boxes down and handed a clipboard to me. I caught view of Mickey leaning against a trolley full of wooden crates, smoking a cigarette. He couldn't see me from where he was, we had a big garden in front of our house and he was all the way at the end.

I signed the clipboard whilst awkward silence buzzed in the background. I was so squirmish all of a sudden, I handed it back to him. I decided it would only be polite if I started a conversation.

"So, you have a job?"

"Yeah, Monday through to Friday." He really does have a wonderful smile. It shifts his whole face.

"Oh, so you don't go to school?" He shook his head.

"How strange."

He pushed his hair out of his eyes, "You look really pretty today."

"Oh...yeah. I mean, thank you."

Mickey shouted at Keith from the distance, begging him to hurry up.

"The total is eight hundred by the way." Right! I forgot to take the money from the counter. I slipped back into the house and grabbed the envelope off the table. I jotted down my phone number on a piece of paper and placed it in the envelope. Why not?

<u>Alice</u>

Dear Timmy,

When you came back home for your January break, you were in a good mood. I would always try to please you when you came back, by buying you your favourite chocolate or doing something different with my hair. The stupid childish things I did for you soon became one of the few ways that affection was displayed in our relationship. Maybe it was our brains telling us to slow down, we did so many "grown up things" together as kids but never actually made an effort to have a proper relationship. Listen, it's understandable because we were kids so once you have sex with somebody you assume that means you love each other. But what if we didn't love each other at all? I think that surely, I do love you now. But what is this so-called love based on?

Well, when you came home for your January break you hadn't noticed all the effort I put into the house, which upset me at the time. Not to mention although you always say how much you missed me when you were away, you'd never even kiss me upon your arrival. You'd hug me like I was a child, and I always felt so small and useless in your arms. We discussed simple things upon your arrival, like the weather and how your work was in Cape Town. I was so proud to be dating a sailing instructor because that meant something, it meant more than anything I did myself.

Crime was already pretty serious on the island all those years ago. Remember, a couple of months before you came when a boy was murdered? They never quite figured out what happened, but even now I'm sure they haven't. They don't resolve things like that on the island, they leave everything as is, or they make it worse.

Love, Alice

<u>Keith</u>

Sometimes, I think I hate myself. I mean, work only started at quarter to seven but I wake up at four every day. It's actually quite therapeutic I guess, waking up before the sun did. After I got up I had to take a bath, brush my hair and teeth and put on clothes. Usually jeans and an old T-shirt. I have a pair of old All-Stars. They're basically like socks, they're so run down. Lanky religiously gets up at six every day, makes breakfast too. That morning it was mangoes, bread and some hot coffee. Which was every food item we had left.

"You ready for work?" he asked between sips of coffee.

"Yes Sir." He nodded his head.

"You're starting to look all grown up now Keith."

I mean, I guess. I was still skinny as a damn twig though, still had that dumb piggish nose of mine. I say it like you can grow out of a nose.

"You know Keith, if you have a girlfriend or somebody you're interested in romantically or whatsoever you should tell me."

I nodded my head, shoved the remaining bread in my pocket and walked up to him. I'm sure that he's over two metres tall. I stood on tip-toes and flicked him on the forehead "You should tell me too."

His eyebrows rose and disappeared into his hair. "What does that mean, kid?"

"Nothing, I'm not the one getting random love letters in the mail that's all." I raised my hands up in an overdramatic shrug, impressed at the speed of my comeback.

Before he could respond I ran out the door, Mickey was as drunk as can be last night. He wasn't a fun guy when he was hungover. A little bit of coffee and I was fine. I couldn't say I remembered much of the night before after walking those girls home though.

Mickey's house was this shack covered by trees. When Alice was still around, we painted it with him. Still has the paintings, the peace sign, a tree and all that. His door was open. So I went straight to the back and he was still in bed, next to Lotus. I wonder how he got home last night and how long he was with that kid and his sister, but I didn't ask because I didn't want to worry Lotus. I didn't want to wake her either so I walked into his room, over the clothes and poked at his head.

"Keith, the fuck you doing?" Mickey is not a morning person.

I jolted slightly because he gave me a fright. He looked like a dead body a second ago. I clear my throat, because he hates that sound when he's hungover. "We have jobs, remember?"

Mickey stretches his body out and lets out an overexaggerated yawn, then kisses Lotus on the cheek. He then belts out: "Left a good job in the city, working for the man every night and day." In the ugliest Tina impression I've ever heard. He was a horrible singer, I don't know how Lotus could sleep through that torture.

We finished work at about half past five, headed to Mr Rain's office. It's a small little shack built right on the stretch of beach we got on our side. Of course our stretch of beach is a rocky, broken beer glass filled mess compared to the other one. There were lots of little shacks built on the taller boulders. Houses, a bar, a restaurant and some take-away joints. This kid Skippy worked in the office, we counted the money and checked the order list. He also hung up flyers on the weekends. This girl, Thandi who was about twenty also worked in the office. She made the calls and wrote down addresses for us. She used to date Mickey some time ago, but they broke it off. Actually, Lotus might be the first girl that Mickey was ever serious about besides Thandi. He never quite told me why Thandi left him, he probably cheated but that's none of my business. Anyway, Mr Rain wasn't with us, he was always on his boat that sat stupid in the marina. He cleaned that thing practically every day, it never went anywhere.

We walked into the damp, cold office. Thandi had ordered four parcels of fish and chips for us. They were laid out on the table, Skippy had already started but Thandi being the genuine person that she is always waited until we were all back. Mickey and I plonked ourselves down on the couch and he handed Thandi the clipboard.

Mickey looks over at Thandi and says: "Mr and Mrs Lee insist that they ordered a bottle of wine so we gotta bring them one tomorrow."

Skippy and I gorged ourselves on the food. Thandi, who loved to press Mickey's buttons waited a while before responding. She popped a chip in her mouth, chewed real slow, licked all her fingers and whipped them off with a cloth before responding.

"Well, make sure you charge them for it." Thandi half mumbles, keeping real intense eye-contact with him for some reason. Like they both knew something that we didn't.

"Wait a second, who delivered food to Mr and Mrs Radebe?" Skippy asks, with one chip in his hand and another opening a piece of paper. Mr and Mrs Radebe, those were Odette's parents. I was glad she answered the door instead of somebody else, seeing her kinda made my whole day better. I don't even know why, It's weird I know.

"I did, why?" I asked, distracted cause I realised a blue bruise on Skippy's arm.

Skippy got up and stood on the table which made Mickey and Thandi stop arguing and look over at him.

"Is this kid drunk or what?" Mickey asked, nudging Thandi with his shoulder.

"Oh Keith! I think the mom has the hots for you!" Skippy yells and starts making the most disturbing movements I've ever seen which must be what a fifteen year old kid thinks of as a dirty joke.

I crawled up on the table and tried to snatch the note from him but he turned his hand and passed it to Mickey.

"Shit Keith, there's a phone number on here!" Mickey started laughing hysterically. Thandi, who was fed up walked over to Mickey and snatched the letter. She passed it to me.

"Jesus guys, it's not from the mom it's from the daughter." I said, but I didn't believe it entirely. Does she like me?

"Heck, maybe I should do one of these delivery jobs." Skippy jumped down from the table and started picking at my food.

"You'd scare the customers away." Thandi says kinda dryly and sits down on Mickey's lap. Mickey doesn't even flinch, like it's a normal thing for her to do.

"What the hell she giving you her number for?" Mickey asked, more amused than concerned. I guess, in his brain this number was a good thing because he thought I was gay, which seemed to be such a big worry for him. But me, well that number meant I finally had a chick who was actually interested in me, and a rich one too. Not saying money matters in a chick, but it's nice to know that she doesn't think I'm complete trash.

"You know what Keith, you keep your letter and we'll take the money. It's time to close up shop anyhow. Keith walk Skippy home please, Mickey and I are going to stay here and uh...finish up some work," Thandi says.

Huh, since when did Mickey and Thandi close up the shack together. You don't even need two people to do that. Weak ass excuse for whatever they were actually doing. God, I don't even wanna know.

<u>Lanky</u>

Out of the thirty something people that got some booze from our store, at least ten of them were like, twelve years old. Ten! Mickey says we should let them buy because nobody else will so we'll make money off of it. Lotus helps me with the whiskey bottles, we mix half of them with water, the kids can't tell the difference. I closed up shop early that day, took all the left over bottles and put them in boxes under the counter. I threw a sheet over the counter and grabbed the cash we made. I took the cooler boxes and dumped the ice outside. Now it just looked like a regular old garage, not a poison factory.

Keith was laying in his room, what a sad room I'd provided him with. A thin small mattress on the ground, some band posters, a homemade clothing rack. July was in four months, I would need to stitch up his winter jacket. I gave him one hundred rand and told him to run to the market to pick up some things we needed. "You can keep the change, kiddo." He smiled that smile of his and said something about going out tonight with a friend. I told him it was fine, as long as he came back home quietly.

He left almost immediately, I should cut his hair soon. Shit, I should cut my own hair soon. I sat on my bed and suddenly became aware of that feeling, where your body is moving aimlessly around and your brain is just sitting, stewing, pickling. I dialed her number on the landline. I spent all day rehearsing in my mind what I would say but hadn't expected to feel as empty as I did, as I do, as I always am when I think about her, or read those letters. Each sharp ring made my hands weaker and weaker, weaker and weaker, weaker and weaker.

"Hello." I'd know that voice from a mile away.

"Alice?" I heard her sigh and shift a bit.

"Timmy." I was crying all of a sudden. At once I felt this, release of all this messy shit I carry around with me constantly. Hot tears down my cheeks and snot in my nose and heat on my forehead and dryness in my throat. All of it at once, so silently. There I was crying in the corner of my room. Like when I was a little boy, I had promised myself never to do that again and there I was.

"Hey Alice, how have you been?" My voice was surprisingly monotone.

"Oh Timmy, oh god, oh my god." She started quietly sobbing into the phone. Her voice was exactly the same. It felt like listening to a used memory.

"I'm doing well, I suppose. I don't have much complaints about anything, it's...you know, normal" She continued.

"Yeah, is it cold that side? I'm sure it's really windy." Why did I sound so fake?

"Oh, yes the wind is strong. It blew over the rubbish bin this morning actually. Vicky and I had to pick it up and everything." She sounded happy, more content than I remember.

"Who's Vicky?"

"My roommate. Goodness Timmy I have so much to tell you, don't I? I have no doubt you feel the same. Hold on a minute I'm in the kitchen, I'm going to move to my bedroom quickly." I could hear her footsteps pattering on the floor. I can hear short and anxious breaths. She did have asthma, I wonder if it got better or worse?

"Where are you right now, Timmy?" She let out a little yawn as she spoke.

"Oh, I'm in our room, by the landline." She laughed. My god did I miss her laugh.

"I forgot that island is stuck in the nineteen hundreds. Why don't you lie on the bed? I'm lying on my bed right now." I haven't been on that bed since she left, four years ago. I haven't touched that bed in four years, it still has a crease in it from when she last sat down. Maybe I imagined that.

"Ok, sure." The landline cord could stretch just enough to reach the pillow on the left side of the bed. I laid myself kinda stiffly on the right side.

"What side are you laying on?" She asked.

"Right."

"Ok." She shifted a little. "I'm lying on the left side now, I've got the phone on the pillow on the right side." She yawned again.

"Oh, so technically I'm lying next to you." I said.

"Yeah, I guess so."

"Can we stay like this for a little while?"

"I'd like that, I'd like that very much."

<u>Odette</u>

Mama was taking photographs of me the whole day to post on my Instagram page, which I don't have access to but that's because it's strictly for work and not for personal use. I haven't had any sponsors or proper modelling jobs since I got here and Mama says it's because I gained five kgs. She's usually very fixed on what my body looks like but that day she was particularly focused on my face and what I should get done to it when I turn eighteen. A rhinoplasty, baby Botox and buccal fat removal for starters were her main suggestions. I've always been called pretty and I suppose most people would think that I was so, but whenever I look at my face I feel indifferent. Not pretty, not ugly, not two ways about everything. But, I suppose I felt that was about most things.

Sometime after Mama went for a run, I heard a knock on the door. I pulled the door open just a touch and gasped as some kind of jerk-reaction. Keith! I closed the door shut quickly. I turned my head, looked down the corridor. White marble, everything white marble, Tata and I joke that Mama picked the house because she could blend in with the background. She probably could. I opened the door again, he was still standing there, wearing a blue shirt that he didn't button up at all and exposed a faint tattoo on his collar bone "fuck it" it read. Very odd contrast to the smile with mouth framing dimples. I slipped outside and shut the door behind me. Tip toed on the grass next to our driveway.

"Hey, I didn't kno-"

"SHHHHHHHHHHHHH."

He moved closer and bent down so that his lips were right by my left ear.

"Hey, I didn't know you were busy. I thought we could take a walk, it's full moon tonight ya know? There's a party by the beach I reckon, even if there isn't...would be nice to talk."

Would it be? I suppose this was his awkward way of asking me out on a date. Maybe he hasn't dated anybody before. I didn't know if I wanted to go out with him, I thought he was relatively good looking and sweet, but there are a lot of relatively good-looking and sweet people out there. Not to mention Mama and Tata would not be impressed if I was going out alone with a boy let alone somebody with the...appearance and financial stature that Keith displayed. Plus, worst case scenario he could actually be a terrible person like a murderer or something. But that's too far-fetched. I was at a crossroads, and the longer I think on this situation the more I begin to freak him out as I'm staring right at him. I looked over once more at the tattoo on his collarbone, he was right.

<u>Keith</u>

My guess was that she had strict parents. She was all nervous when I got to her door, like I wasn't allowed to be there or she wasn't allowed to be out. It kinda bugs me, but Lanky says I shouldn't ask people about their business. She was all of a sudden in a different mood, more adventurous holding my hand and skipping along. Her eyes kept on circling back to the stick-and-poke Mickey gave me. I was so pissed with him that day, I told him to just "get it over and done with" so he wrote fuck it on my collarbone. What a real prince Mickey is. A real prince.

Odette was looking around at the sky that was inky and glossy with light coverage of the clouds. We weren't talking but for some reason it wasn't that awkward. We were pretty peaceful in our silence. I kept on looking at the slope of her perfect nose.

"You got a nice nose." Shit, wasn't supposed to say that aloud.

She looked over at me and smiled. "Thanks."

The party had less people which was nice, some of Skippy's friends were there and a couple of other kids. The only older people who were there was Mickey, Thandi, Mickey's old dealer and some chicks. Mickey's eyes seemed relived as soon as he saw me. It was dark now and the big fire in the middle was the only source of light besides the beaming moon. Some people did a double take because I was walking with Odette.

Mickey half smiled at Odette and turned to look at me. "Listen man, have you seen Lotus anywhere?" I shrugged.

"Where have you been Mousey Man?"

He turned to look back at Thandi who was walking in the water with some other chicks.

"Oh, nothing to worry about kiddo." Hmmm. Something was definitely up, but I was too lazy to care. I walked Odette over to the boulder that was kinda hidden by this palm tree. She stretched herself over it, her glinting eyes danced off the moonlight. She was smiling. As cheesy as it sounds, she made me feel different, I don't know. Special for some reason. Looked at.

"I really like you," she said. I laid myself down next to her.

"Oh really?"

"Yeah, I guess that's weird since we've only met like, twice."

"I mean yeah but, I'm a pretty nice guy wouldn't ya say? Some would even call me, a catch." She laughed and turned to look at me.

"Tell me about yourself, your parents, where you're from."

"Here, always been here." I shrugged and dug in my pocket for a smoke.

"Oh, what's your ethnicity? Because you don't look like most of the native islanders around here that I've seen." She used big words that made me stop and think for a bit before responding, which was both interesting and annoying. It kind of reminds me of Alice. But at least with Alice, she would explain the words to me and try to make me use them when I spoke.

"Uh, my mom was Chinese." I didn't like taking about her. It made my hands shake. I stood up and held my jittery hand out to her. She grabbed it and we walked down together. Mickey was with Lotus. They were chilling with the others along the shore. I don't know where the music came from. It was a little too loud though. So off we went, through the palm trees, across the harbour, past the stalls down to my house. I came in quietly and went upstairs. Odette was behind me. We sat on my bed. "So this is your house?" I nodded my head. "Yeah I live here with my uhhh, uncle I guess. Lanky" She smiled and asked about the posters. She was real nice about the whole thing. I know my house wasn't as nice as what she was used to. Soon though, I thought. I'd have a big old house like hers soon.

We talked for hours I bet, about pretty much everything. Talked about all the places she visited and I told her about the tattoo. She had a nice laugh. When the sun started to come up we decided it was time for her to get home. I walked her to the Mountain Pass and kissed her goodbye. I watched her half run half walk back. When she faded away I turned home. To be honest, I hate kissing. Like, what's the point of it anyway? Why can't you like somebody, and tell them you like them. I don't like touching, it feels invasive most of the time. When I told Mickey, he said I'd understand when I grew up. Thing is, I'm all grown up now and I still don't understand.

<u>Alice</u>

Dear Timmy,

Back then, life was better for me when you weren't around. I had this friend, Miranda who was talking about moving to Cape Town. This sounded nice to me, I always imagined that once you saved up enough money from your job we'd move there permanently. Miranda, who is always very honest to the point of being blunt told me that I needed to learn that I can't always depend on other people. I didn't understand her at the time, I thought she just didn't understand how relationships work but maybe she was right, I did always depend on other people. And you only depend on yourself.

Well, something else I never told you was that before I moved to the island I did ballet. I was serious about it too, en pointe and everything. But my love for dance proved to be too expensive for my mother after the divorce. After we moved to the island, it felt like everything was on hold and I had always imagined we'd be leaving soon but we never did. When she died, when she left me alone I threw myself into our relationship. I guess I did this for some sort of comfort. What I'm trying to say is, that year on your January break before Keith even came into the picture I wanted to leave the island. But I never told you that because you were too busy for me, and all I ever did was wait for you to come home.

Love, Alice

<u>Lanky</u>

Alice and I had been talking every day. It felt nice to talk to somebody, I didn't talk to people that much. All my old friends had moved on, moved off the island. Started new lives elsewhere. That was never my plan. I didn't think that far ahead, I didn't live in the moment or in the past. I just, existed without much passion for anything. Alice was basically the only person I talked to, properly. We both had the same experiences, her mother passed on around the same time as my grandmother. That's how we met actually, at the graveyard behind the palm trees.

My grandmother died of pneumonia. I hadn't lived with her for too long, I was sent over after my father got custody. He wasn't a great guy, he used to hit my mom around a lot. He beat her so hard one time that she blacked out, I sat there and watched. I always did, I never protected her the way I should have. Then with my grandmother too, never protected her. I didn't care for her enough. Maybe she would have gotten better if I looked after her a little more. What's great about Alice is, she lets me take care of her. She understands, even when we first started going out. It's difficult to have a genuine connection with somebody nowadays. If you do, you're a fool to let it go.

Well, I hadn't spoken to anybody about it yet. That's why I was lying on my bed staring at the leaky ceiling. Reading her latest letter, which is actually kinda difficult for me to get through all at once because it was so...critical. Alice and I planned to meet, planned for me to visit her in Cape Town. With my savings it wouldn't be too much. I know this guy Thulani, he had a little boat that he takes out to Cape Town once a month. I could ask to get a ride with him, it's about one day at a slow pace. I had to buy some food and water but it wasn't be too expensive. Alice said that when I got there I could stay with her for a bit. I figured I would find a job to get me by. I wanted to bring Keith with but I would have to sedate him before he would go on a boat to leave the island. He got skidish when boats went too far away from the land. I only wanted to go for a month or two, then come back. I hadn't really thought that long term about it, Alice and I didn't really know where we stood. It's complicated. You don't know how often I think thought about her dating other guys. It freaked me out.

The door swang open and I could hear Mickey talking. Interrupting my thoughts as per usual. It was Friday, which usually meant date night for him and Lotus. They had to schedule because Lotus was a really hard worker so she kept herself busy. Waitressing and helping out at Stall Street. I thought she was very admirable, constantly pushing Mickey to be more motivated. They argued constantly but to be honest, I didn't know a single person who didn't constantly argue with Mickey. I suppose him and Keith didn't argue that much, simply because those two were basically blood brothers. Mickey walked into the room, his short frame leaned against the door. Besides the smell of weed, he cleaned himself up quite a bit, washed his hair and put on a nice shirt. Then I realised something...

"Hey, are you wearing my shirt?"

He nodded his head. "It's green Lank, suits my angelic eyes don't ya think." Sometimes Keith talked just like him. He still does, but it's more rare now.

"Well, Big Ears, that has nothing to do with anything but, you can borrow it for today." I had no intention in fighting with Mickey, he was one of those people that never lost an argument because he made you talk in circles until you were so exhausted, you just agreed with him.

He laid down on the bed next to me. He made himself at home way too easily. I sat up in slight discomfort, I could smell his perfume, kind of sweet and floral.

"Are you wearing women's perfume?"

"So what if I am? Besides, Lotus says I need to work on my "toxic masculinity." Whatever the hell that means."

I rolled my eyes. "Your stupidity never ceases to amaze me. Anyway, can I tell you something?"

He grinned. "Yeah man, I'm all ears."

"You certainly are."

"Are you gonna tell me or not?"

So I told him everything, he was a surprisingly good listener. Nodding his head the whole time, never loosing eye contact. He really did have piercing eyes, they dug deep into the back of your brain. They used to freak me out actually, until I got to know him. After I told him, he mulled over it for a little bit. Scraping his tongue over his teeth. A habit he was known for. The wind made the house scream and whine, tension was building. I think he thought I was an idiot for wanting to see Alice, but he didn't show it.

"I mean, I don't know Lank. If you're like one hundred percent sure you want to, do it. I'll stay here with Keith so he'll be fine. I hope you've talked enough with her though, because that chick made you fuckin depressed. So, don't be surprised if she makes you feel that way again. And, she's probably been with other guys. You haven't been with anybody because you're too attached, man. So try and be more chill when you see her. What I'm trying to say is, it's not going to be the same. You and Alice split up right after you got Keith right? And...you still got Keith. So how do you know that she's gonna be ok with that? All I'm saying is, be careful man. "

Odette

As I walked up our walkway to the front door I felt uneasy. I knew that I would get into trouble but how bad could it be? I got in trouble with them all the time, I shouldn't have to avoid doing fun things because I'm scared of them. What type of person would I become? Ok, I thought. The worst thing that could happen is a hiding and maybe extra exercises. Then I took a second to look around. First warning, the lights were all off. Second, it was about five in the morning. Third, the door swung open before I even knocked. Tata was standing there, looming over me in the dark.

He didn't say anything, because of course not. He grabbed my wrists and dragged me inside the house. Numb, I thought. Just to make myself numb for these few minutes and I'd be ok. He shoved me on the ground and I hit the back of my head. Then without a word, without even the slightest hesitation he kicked me over and over on my sides. The pain hugged my ribs. I tried my best not to make any noise because I knew that would make the situation much worse. He stopped after a while, when these things happen it's best to pretend that you're in a movie. Like you're just watching it happen. It stopped after a while, I'm not too sure when but he had left. I was falling in and out of consciousness.

Of course Mama was there the whole time, watching from the kitchen. She walked up to me and lifted me up. Then she grabbed my face and examined it, her long nails digging into my cheeks. Her face was even paler than usual, she looked like a skull. Even her eyes looked like dark voids. That's why she usually wore blue contacts. Her sharp nose, like a dagger inches away from my forehead. "You smell like cigarettes." She stood up. "Oh don't be dramatic Odette, everybody gets disciplined it's part of growing up." My eyes struggled to stay open, my eyelids felt like they weighed a million tons. I felt wishy washy, my brain fading away into itself. The floor, it was melting, turning into a white cold liquid. Like quicksand, I was falling into it and swirling around endlessly in a circle. I clawed my hands and tried to grasp it, it was impossible. My hands were blending in with the whiteness. My arms, my legs, my whole body until only my head was left. As I tried to gasp for air, the floor began to spill into my rib cage. Making its way in-between the cracks, spilling its liquid cold pain all over. I began to sink into the ground, deeper and deeper and deeper.

Keith

I had that dream again, that dream I kept on having over and over again, after my parents dipped. Blood. Blood in the water. Spreading across the island. Combing it's droopy fingers through the sand. Swallowing. Consuming. Looking for me. Hunting. Tearing down all the fancy houses, tearing down the palm trees. Spilling through the Mountain Pass. Stripping away at the wooden shacks. We're trying to swim through it but it's too thick, we can taste it as it spills into our mouths. We're too tired now, so we stop fighting it. We let it take us away, red washes over my eyes and then I wake up.

Lanky was awake and at the table already, my eyes were barely open I was so damn tired. I sat down at the table, he already made breakfast and coffee so all I had to do was sit down and eat. He stood opposite me, looking at me with this weird expression of sad and happy. "Hey kid, once you're done with work we need to talk ok?" He stiffly patted me on the shoulder. "Ja ok," I said, walking out of the door. I was late already. I wish I didn't have to go to work and I could go see Odette or something. Mickey was still at his house I reckon, since we always go together. So I went to his and funny enough he was arguing with Lotus. I walked in slowly and sat in the "living room." Lotus and Mickey must have been fighting in his room or something. I hate hearing people fight it's a really uncomfortable thing. Not like there's people out there who like hearing people fight. All I mean is I can actually get physically nauseous from hearing people fight. People can act different when they're angry and do things they wouldn't normally do, and I really don't like that. I started thinking about my parents, I always did after I have that dream. Lotus walked into the living room, not as angry as I was expecting, she actually walked out of the house rather calmly. She didn't see me though, then Mickey walked out of his room all sad like he's about to cry. I don't think he's ever cried in front of me.

"Come kid, we're uh, late for work." He tucked his messy brown hair behind his ears and looked at me.

"Shit man, I know you don't like it but you really do look like your mom."

"Stop doing that."

He sighed, walking out of the door without seeing if I was following. I half walked half ran to him. Wondering why him and Lotus were fighting, so I asked.

"Adult stuff Keith."

"I am an adult."

"Well ok adult. I don't want to dive into the specifics of my relationships with you. It's not something that you need to know. Stop being so fuckin nosey all the time."

"Damn, ok." I don't know why everybody was acting so weird all of a sudden. Plus, I wasn't nosey. The whole reason why Mickey and I were so close was because I didn't bother him with questions like other people did. He usually told me everything I needed to know anyhow. I was the one who didn't tell him stuff. I didn't tell him things that I should've.

We got to Mr Rain's shack but it was closed. Locked up. Lights off. Empty. Skippy, Thandi, Mickey and I all stood around the shack staring blankly. Thandi motioned for Mickey to come to her and they had one of their whisper talks that were becoming too frequent. "Shit." I said, trying to full the silence. Skippy said that his grandparents heard that Mr Rain was leaving but didn't wanna believe it until he saw for himself. Shit, out of work. What the hell were we all supposed to do. We all needed those jobs. I needed to make some extra cash, I knew that Lanky had been struggling some and I promised to help him out. I hate breaking promises. Especially to somebody like Lanky who doesn't deserve that type of crap. He had enough stress.

"Could have at least told us, the bastard," Skippy yelled. He picked up a rock and threw it at the trashy shack. Made a loud PANG and hit the ground in front of me. Was like that sound was echoing, ringing in my ears.

"If he dipped then I will too." I said, turning myself and leaving. The sight of his shack was making me real angry which is not an emotion I could handle very well.

I figured Odette would make me feel better. Odette, Odette and her rich girl smile. Odette who smelled like pearl necklaces and fresh mimosas (I dunno, fancy stuff). I never knew you could want to make somebody smile or laugh so badly. Attention, that's probably it. I wanted her attention, funny I never cared much for attention since there wasn't such a high supply of it when I was a kid. There I go again thinking about when I was a kid. Sometimes I swim too much in my own head and when I get out I'm somewhere completely different. There I was in front of the Mountain Pass. Stepping into the rich side always felt weird. The sun hit on that side much faster, it looked brighter. All the different houses, massive. Like a mansion or that house in the one movie that played in that bar. The Great Gatsby. I think Odette's house was like that. But, I try not to think about her house anymore. With the big gardens and rich people doing rich people things. They don't have to worry about losing their jobs. Got so much money they could build a little chair made out of hundred rand bills and sit on it. Like some obnoxious politician, or a villain in a movie. God, where is my brain.

I walked up Odette's massive driveway and knocked on the door. I was suddenly aware of how worn down my jeans are, how my big naked feet were bruised on the sides. What the hell happened to my pinkie toenail? It was clean off, a pink fleshy stub. A woman opens the door, pale and slim. She had hair the same colour as Alex's but it was straight and sharp. Like somebody had chopped it off with a machete. Her nose was real thin and nice, like Odette's. She had thin lips with red lipstick. The only colour noticeable since she was so damn pale and her clothes were white. She must be the whitest looking white person I ever saw. I guess Mickey was also pretty white but he never admitted it.

"Who are you?" She had an accent, I couldn't really tell where from.

I cleared my throat and tried to fix my slouch which made my back crack real loud. Awkward.

"Hi, uh...I'm Keith. Odette's uh... friend."

She looked oddly uncomfortable, looked at me like I was something gross she left in the trash to rot but suddenly grew legs and crawled back to her feet. Odette creeped up from behind. She looked different, he eyes looked smaller for some reason. She didn't look at me the same way she usually does, she looked at me like how this pale lady was looking at me.

"I'm sorry Mama this is the boy that delivers food. I forgot to tip him." She disappeared again and her mom closes the door a little more narrowly. I should have known it was her mom, I'm so dumb sometimes. Odette came back and handed me fifty rand then told me to leave. It was weird, like it wasn't even Odette talking. It suddenly felt like I was watching that rich people movie unfold right in front of me. I can tell when somebody doesn't want me around, so I nodded and left. Incredibly embarrassed and feeling a thousand times more terrible then I felt before.

When I got back home I shut the door behind me. I looked down the front of the house but couldn't see the lights of the alcohol shop on. Lanky must have been having a sick day or something. I opened up the scrunched up fifty rand and there was a note inside.

"Don't come here, ever." It read. I chucked it on the floor. It wasn't that her parents were strict it's that they thought I was trash and she didn't want to embarrass her family. Sometimes I hate things about myself, things I want to change but it's real hard. It's not fair when you're born with something that makes people hate you. I was trying my best to change it but it wasn't happening fast enough. I hated the way people looked at me, without even realising they were looking at me like that. Looking at me like I was absolute filth that they felt bad for. Looking at me with pity, like their pity could change a goddamn thing.

Lanky called me to his room and made me sit on his bed next to him. He was always real warm, like he had this warm air kinda bounce off him when you sat close. His eyes were smiling, my god did he have the strangest shape shifting eyes. At that moment they were like honey, all warm and sweet. Which was rare, most times they looked grey and dead, like he was thinking about something far away. People tell me that my eyes look like that now, but back then they didn't used to. Maybe it comes with age. Lanky started talking for a while. Started on about me and what a "good kid" I was. He always takes long to get to the point. Finally, he told me. He was going over to Cape Town for a month for some work. He said Mickey would be staying here with me. "I know the month is over in a couple days. So when you get paid you don't have to give me half just keep it for yourself. That should be enough right? Just you know, don't spend it all. I know I don't have to worry about that with you though." He squeezed my hand, then mumbled an apology because he knows I don't like that stuff. He's very touchy feely sometimes. I didn't tell him about the job, I couldn't. I knew that the only thing I could do was get another one. I had to. Then it would be fine.

Mickey came in sometime in the evening. He told me that he wanted to talk. I didn't wanna talk at all, I felt like shit. Lanky's leaving, Odette and her parents think I'm trash and I officially don't have a job. Mickey kind of insists though, his eyes looked real harsh. I followed him, he was walking fast. Past the green shack, past the braai spot, past Stall Street all the way down to that fish and chips spot. "So you're taking me out on a date, huh?" He didn't respond to the joke. The restaurant had a few people here and there with the TV playing some old timey film in the corner. The restaurant was a bit of a dump but it was the only restaurant on our side. There were no plates and fancy silver spoons like at the place Lotus works at. At the back, Thandi and Skippy were sitting on one of the sticky wooden benches. Skippy is sucking Coke out of a broken straw.

I sit down next to Skippy and look over at Mickey and Thandi. Mickey and Thandi are looking at each other and then Mickey nods. I started to feel a little freaked out by their silence but Skippy was too distracted by the coke leaking out of his straw. He was real good at doing small irritating things all the time.

Thandi started on this speech:

"Listen kids, we all knew that Mr Rain was a good for nothing bastard didn't we?" The whole table nodded their heads with bitter agreement. "Can we blame him? If we had enough money we'd leave this shit hole too, wouldn't we? How can we make enough money to do that? Look at us, we're at the bottom of the barrel. Even the charity places stopped coming around. Nobody wants us! We've all been working our asses off since we were kids for what? Our good for nothing parents to do fockall? To keep our little shitty houses afloat? The only people who have a chance are people who think smart. This work hard and you'll succeed shit is bull."

Mickey was looking straight at me the whole time, not saying anything. His green eyes studying me. Like a snake behind a bush, watching the innocent lamb for slaughter. So still, all the muscles in his face completely relaxed. This speech was definitely planned. I looked over at Skippy who was barely phased, drinking his coke and nodding along.

Thandi grabbed both out our hands and lowered her voice and head. "Those people on the other side? They don't have to worry about anything. They're taking over our island with their fancy houses and restaurants. Their massive mansions insured so they're never affected by anything bad. They don't know what it's like for people like us. Hell, they don't care! I know how they look at you guys, like you're stray animals. It's time we show them!" She let go of our hands and looked at Mickey. Her dark eyes soaked with frustration and pride. I wasn't too sure what we had to "show them" but clearly Thandi was a little sauced because she wasn't usually this expressive.

"Skip, Keith I know you guys are angry. I'm fuckin angry myself. Look at us! We're out of work. We need the money kids, we're all fucking starving, we're all fucking depressed, we're all fucking miserable. Those rich assholes have never known what's it's like to suffer, they have it good. On our fucking island! Thandi and I want to help you guys, we want to help each other. Here's the plan:"

They started talking about this one house on the rich side that an old English couple use as a holiday house. They said they've been monitoring it for a while and apparently they only come on Christmas. They said the house is close to that big palm tree, a little secluded. It had big windows and no fences and it was full of expensive shit. They wanted us to all break in and steal. Just a few things, not enough to notice or cause a big deal.

"Listen guys, nobody is there. We wouldn't be hurting anybody. We go in, we take some stuff and Thandi and I handle the rest, turn it into cash. We'll split it evenly between the four of us, nobody will know. Nobody is even going to care ok?"

Skippy leaned back in his chair. "I mean ja, that could work. But, we need a plan. Maybe some supplies."

"Well James Bond, Thandi and I will sort all that out. You two just have to pitch up on the night. That's all. Are you guys in?" Mickey hadn't taken his eyes off me since he started talking. I didn't know what to think, I've always told him I don't like being involved with that type of crap. But, we needed the money. It wasn't supposed to hurt anyone, and I trusted Thandi and Mickey.

"Ok, I'm in." I said, Mickey immediately broke eye contact and smiled at Thandi. He had this "I told you so" look on his face. "I'm in too," said Skippy. The plan was for us to meet tomorrow at Mickey's. They wanted us to move fast and do the job this weekend.

On the walk home, I felt weird. I couldn't stand all the illegal shit Mickey was constantly trying to shove on me, I didn't like doing the wrong thing. But it felt safe, a way to make some money. If we did a couple of those sort of things, I thought I could have save up enough to get out of this place. Just like Thandi said, buy myself a new life. Maybe go back to school, get a place to stay. Be one of those guys in the films with the fancy suits and the gelled hair. Then I could go up to Odette's house and knock on the door. Her mother would smile "Who is this handsome young man?" Odette would run up to me and give me a hug. Look at her mother proudly and say "This is my boyfriend." Then we'd go inside and they'd treat me like a real respectable guy. I'd say things like "Well I'm studying business at blah blah blah university." I'd be all respected and rich then I'd be happy.

It's still crime I guess, no matter how pure the intention. So I won't keep it up for too long. You can't cheat at life, even if life cheats you.

<u>Alice</u>

Dear Timmy,

When you were off work for the Easter holidays, we had a lot more time to spend together. You kept on bringing up the fact that my birthday was coming up soon because we had no other surface level bullshit to talk about. We kept on having arguments about the smallest things, most of which were started by me. Everything you did began to irritate me, the way you chew, the sound of your breath while you're sleeping, the way you randomly hum made up tunes. I thought I was the bad buy because on paper you're the perfect boyfriend. You never forget anniversaries, birthdays and things of that nature. Christ, you made me breakfast in bed every morning. You always put my needs first, or at least you thought you did. But sometimes, you made me feel like some sort of doll. I must be quiet, pretty, laugh at all your jokes and never disagree. Then you parade me around to all your friends. "Oh right! You're Lanky's girl, aren't you?" I hated that nickname everybody called you. I hated being called "Lanky's girl." It was at that moment, that I knew we needed to break up.

Love, Alice

<u>Odette</u>

Keith took me out to a bar last night, which was actually more fun than I expected but I was not looking forward to it initially. Not because being with Keith wasn't fun but because the bar looked dingy and unsafe. Most, if not all of the people sitting there were middle aged men but that ended up being a prime source if entertainment as we could eavesdrop their conversation.

"You see that guy over there." Keith pointed at some older black guy sitting on a stool crunching on an ice cube.

"His kid was killed like, a couple years back. Nobody ever figured out who did it."

"How was the kid killed?" I asked, with sudden interest.

"Shot in the face, that guy was involved in some sort of gang in Joburg. Moved here to escape, but people found him. I'm pretty sure the police were bribed and that's why they say the case in unsolved." Keith said too casually. If only I picked up on those subtle details sooner, things could have been different.

"Do things like this happen all the time?"

"No, I mean people don't get killed all the time. But people get jumped and beat up quite a bit over here. It's just the way things are, the way people are over here. Not because they're aggressive, they just do what they gotta do. Almost everyone here is like that."

"I don't think you'd ever hurt anybody Keith, you're not like that." I assured him, it was my honest truth. He nodded his head but didn't say anything.

Then, after a while and quite randomly, he told me that I was the most beautiful person he'd ever meet and that he wishes we were older.

"Why?" I ask, I feared aging.

"Because then we could live together alone, somewhere far from here and other people. That's my dream ya know? I'm gonna be so rich one day that I can buy my own house somewhere far from everybody else and all their bullshit. No responsibilities or worries, no feelings of inferiority. No jealousy no hate. Freedom."

"I like that, I'd like to live somewhere where I could be free."

"Well, I'll be able to find that place for us real soon." He said while he sat up straight and looked directly into my eyes. His eyes scared me, his eyes said a lot more than he did. Even back then, I had a feeling his eyes were a lot more honest than he was.

"Do you promise?" I asked, the question sounded and felt much more serious than I expected.

"I promise, Odette. I promise."

<u>Lanky</u>

Alice and I met at the waterfront mall amongst the rush of people. Cape Town is a humid mess of tourists, locals, street dancers, beggars, windy sea breezes and seagulls. It's beautiful but it's very overwhelming. It's different to the boulders and thick greenery of the island and I seemed to have forgotten all about it even though I used to be here all the time. Well, Alice looked different. She looked cleaner, less fragile like she really had her shit together. I didn't, which kind of made me feel weird, I don't know why it's just not the way I'm used to her. She lived in an apartment in Observatory right in the middle of a busy street with restaurants and bars and cool vintage clothing stores.

Her roommate wasn't home when I got there, she was away for the weekend, apparently so that we could be alone which was very considerate. The apartment was nice, it was like a small house with warm coloured walls, hand woven carpets and decorations that looked like they were collected from all over. Alice's room was down the hall past the kitchen, very neat with a queen sized bed and a bedside table with a laptop and makeup and a silver brush she used when we lived together. I put my backpack down on the foot of the bed.

"Are you tired?" She asked as she wiped my hair out of my eyes. I nodded my head in response. She suggested that we get some rest since it's been a long week, I guess we were avoiding the obvious but sometimes it's better to avoid things.

<u>Keith</u>

Skippy, Thandi, Mickey and me were all at Mickey's place going over the plan for tonight. On the table, they laid out the things we needed and I was in charge of ticking off the list I made. Skippy was supposed to write the list but his handwriting was absolute garbage so it became my job.

Four torches

Four pairs of gloves

A crowbar

A backpack

Two garbage bags

Everything was there on the table including the address and description of the house that Thandi wrote down. We weren't really "dressed for the part" everyone was wearing normal clothes but it's not like we were professionals or anything. Anyway, Thandi went over the plan with Mickey and Skip and me. The idea was to pair up, Mickey and Thandi would go to the upstairs while Skip and I stayed downstairs. In our pairs we could only take like, three things because the whole point is that it shouldn't be noticeable.

"Ja ok, how are we getting in?" Skippy asked. Skippy wasn't a smart kid but he did have a point. Thandi told him that while walking past the house she noticed that it had a back door with a small doggy door at the bottom which Skippy could easily fit through, they also had a window in the bottom floor bathroom so Skip would get into the house and open the bottom floor bathroom door for us and we would climb through.

That wasn't the solid answer I was expecting and half of me was worried that any random person walking past could see us even if it was super late. You never know what can happen. Of course, breaking into houses isn't just some fun weekend activity. I never thought that it was and I had my doubts about the whole thing, but I wasn't sweating with nerves or anything. If it was some sort of hostage situation, then I would have been terrified but it was just something quick that wouldn't hurt anybody. My intention was never to hurt anybody.

It was only when we got there that the nerves kicked in, not just for me but for everybody and we all looked real uncomfortable. I watched as Mickey looked around while we walked to the house which sat looking over the beach. It was a white two story with blue paint around the windows and doors and the roof was flat. The downstairs area had wooden floors which creaked with every step and a lot of nice furniture and shit. "Antique" was the word Thandi kept on using to describe them which basically meant old but also expensive or expensive because it's old.

All the chairs had flowers or birds embroidered into them, one green chair sat in front of an "antique" piano with those pretty and long purple flowers on them, lavenders. It made me sit on the floor next to it and stare, made me forget about what was going on. My mind left Skippy behind while he violently opened and closed different drawers, left Mickey and Thandi upstairs and went back to when I was a little younger. When Alice still lived here and when she taught me how to read better and taught me about flowers and dancing and all the things she liked. I wished she was there, but then I was glad she wasn't because if she found out that I was stealing from people she'd be so disappointed. But then again, if she was here maybe I wouldn't be doing this at all. I think there's different versions of your life depending on whether certain people in your life stay or leave. I wonder what would happen if you'd left the people that stayed and stayed with the people that left.

I went to go help Skippy and we took some fancy silver forks, spoons and knifes. We also saw some weird looking rock that was like a fruit, it was black and boring on the outside but on the inside it had a bunch of beautiful pink crystals in it so we shoved that in the bag. Last thing we took was a small candle stick holder because it was shiny silver and looked real expensive. I whisper shouted out to Mickey and Thandi that we should probably leave. They walked down the creaky stairs with Mickey holding their black bag. We went out the bathroom window again and Mickey made sure to close it behind him, well as best he could. Walking back we took the route by the beach because nobody was there and it was our fastest way out.

"We're rich guys!" shouted Skippy, throwing up his skinny arms and nearly chucking the bag over his head.

"Uhm, not quite, kiddo." Saying "kiddo" made me sound old like Lanky. Walking in the sand, I felt you all my weight drop down to my ankles. It's pretty hard to run in the sand so it's a good thing the robbery was successful because I don't know how fast I would be if I had to run away from somebody. Calling it a robbery seemed dramatic at the time, but anyway. As I was walking with everybody I ended up trailin behind them cause there was something in the water. It was a heap or something but when I get closer and the sand got wetter and easier to walk on, the heap was gone. The water was splashing my ankles and I felt sick. I looked down at my feet and when I lifted them up some liquid stuck to them, like dark thick water. But it wasn't water, it was blood.

I jumped back and fell on my back, who's blood was in the water? I was too weak to stand up, so I used my elbows to help me crawl back to safety. But I was not going fast enough and the water was catching up to me. It couldn't do that. It couldn't let it get to me. I was not going with it. I was not going in there. They couldn't take me with them, I wouldn't let them.

I don't remember what happened after that.

<u>Odette</u>

When I was a little girl and Mama, Tata and I were living in France she used to buy lots of magazines. I would flip through them, particularly the fashion magazines. I would look at the long legged beautiful women wearing the most elegant clothing. They were so mesmerising to me, not because they were beautiful but because they could shapeshift. One page would show the same model, but she was different people in each outfit, a new person with each pose. Was she a glamorous femme fatelle? Was she a business woman? A sports woman. A sensual lady lounging on the beach in a swimming costume. She was all these things. That was so exciting to me, that was something I wanted for myself. I remember telling Mama excitedly that I was going to be a supermodel when I got older and I would wear fancy clothes and be whoever I wanted to be. Now looking back on it, it sounds superficial and I don't feel like anybody but myself when I'm being photographed. There's a thin veil created by clothes and poses but...I don't know. I think I lost interest. I think maybe I didn't want to be anybody anymore. I thought I was going to enjoy living on the island but then I just felt lost. With absolutely nothing to do.

Of course I didn't want to shun Keith the way I did but it was necessary. If I hadn't done that I can't begin to imagine Mama's reaction to Keith and I being...whatever we are. He's a really decent person, he's also funny and genuine. His complements don't feel forced, everything he says, he means. He's also so gentle, even if he doesn't look it he's actually quite soft. I feel awful now that I think about it, I feel like a shitty person. So, I told Mama that I was going on a walk and left. Past the mountain pass, down the path Keith took me on all the way to Lanky's house. It was a strange looking house. Very old, it looked like it used to be very nice some years ago but then plants started growing along the walls and a very noticeable crack formed down the front. It almost seemed as though the plants crawling up the wall were essential in keeping the house from falling apart. Like ropes tying broken shards of wall together.

At first, I thought nobody was home because I didn't get a response when I called but the door was open so I went in anyway. It almost felt like a children's play house where you could see what was meant to be a kitchen and a lounge but they didn't have the right equipment so instead they used boxes and outdoor furniture. Although I had been there before it felt like I was viewing it for the first time, noticing little things that hadn't been there before.

"Hello? Keith?" I called, walking deeper into the house which seemed more eerie with each creak.

"What the hell's going on here?" I nearly screamed from shock and when I turned around I saw Keith's friend Mickey at the door frame. He had a curious look plastered on his face. Leaning against the door frame with a cigarette hanging from his mouth, he offered me one.

"That's alright thank you. Do you have any clue where Keith might be?"

"Ja, he's at my house. Listen why don't you come with me and I can take you to him?"

"Alright." I walked over to him and he slung his arm over my shoulder which made me slightly uncomfortable.

"Ya know, I'm saving to buy a house on the other side. Why don't you tell me a bit about the neighbourhood there?"

"Oh um, ok sure, let me think for a moment. What exactly do you want to know?" I thought that it was strange that he had enough money to buy a house on the other side considering his appearance. But maybe thoughts like that made me sound too much like Mama and Tata.

Alice

Dear Timmy,

Everybody knew about Lina and Tom to some extent. I knew them because Lina was your cousin, although you never spoke to her. Everybody else knew Tom was a drug dealer and that Lina was his wife. I mean, they were kind of infamous considering the number of people who were getting addicted to Tik kept on rising. Everybody thought he was poisoning the island, I'll be honest and say I agree. The rise of addicts, loan sharks, and petty criminals. Things were slowly crumbling around me and you weren't there to pick up the pieces. Well, although everybody knew who Lina and Tom were, few people knew that they had a kid, Keith.

I don't like to think about what happened to them, because it's bloody and gory and unpleasant. But, when the police found their bodies on the shore it was clear that Tom had drowned and Lina had died from blunt trauma to the head. Which means, Tom probably killed her. I wonder if Keith ever thinks about that if it makes him feel guilty.

Well, when the police found the bodies and you were called in I was shocked of course. We had a rare moment of connection, the fear and unease I felt was mirrored in your eyes. You were gone for so long, I thought something horrible was about to happen. I was happy to be home alone, but nobody likes being left in the dark.

Keith

"I'm sorry that I acted that way, Keith I really didn't mean too." Odette explained, not looking at me but at her clasped hands. She came by with Mickey, apparently looking for me at Lanky's.

"Yeah Odette, it's not about whether or not you're sorry. It was a shit thing to do, and I know exactly why you did it." For some reason, the fact that I wasn't looking at her while talking made it much easier to say how I actually felt.

"What do you mean "why I did it"?" Her voice got a little shaky when she was angry. I don't think she should have felt angry, I'm the one who should have felt angry.

"It's because you're ashamed of me. You know, since we're hanging out and whatever. You're ashamed, you don't want your parents to know that you like somebody like me. You think I'm just some pending charity case, and deep down you think you deserve better...your need to please your parents is more than your need to I dunno, your need to be with me I guess."

"I'm not ashamed of you...I just. Well my parents are pretty strict about boyfriends and things like that so I didn't want them to find out like that. But I uh...I spoke to them privately and told them about you." I didn't know she thought of me like that, I had never really had a girlfriend before.

"I'm your boyfriend?"

"I mean, we both like each other right? I just thought...that's the direction we're headed." I nodded my head, I felt a little better about the whole situation. I didn't know if there was some kind of official thing you're supposed to do for somebody to be your girlfriend. I avoided the topic of dating with Lanky, and when I asked Mickey he said: "I dunno man, the chicks just come flying to me." Which wasn't helpful at all.

"Oh...ok. So where are your parents, still home?" The fact that she told her parents about me was real nice.

"Um, they're both away on business right now, they left a couple of hours ago so when they get back in a couple of weeks you can meet them if you want."

I said yes, not realising Odette thought I was that important to her, it felt good because it's nice to feel important to people. I'm not used to feeling important. She decided to change the subject, she asked if I wanted to take a walk by the harbour and I said sure. We ended up walking for a couple of hours, I was happy listening to her talk about whatever popped into her head. I think one of these days when I have money I'll take her someplace real special, but for now walking by the harbour will do me just fine.

<u>Lanky</u>

Being in Cape Town was like living in a cool breeze. The air is sweet and the people are relaxed, the music is entrancing and I felt it pulse through my heart like a drum. Cape Town is like an image of technicolour, flashing blue, green and all sorts of cool hues. I was in a different kind of paradise and I was in it with Alice. It was as though I was falling in love with her again the same way I did all those years ago. Her roommate Vicky was pretty nice although I got the feeling she didn't like me. Almost as if she had already made her mind up about me before we met. Anyway, Alice found a job for me very quickly, working as a garden keep for a family in Constantia. It was a grand mansion overlooking a vineyard. It reminded me of those old movies Keith was so obsessed with. I did miss him a lot...sometimes. To be honest, there were times where I didn't think about him at all like he never existed and I'd always lived with Alice in Cape Town. I think it's just because she was my whole life before Keith. It was only us two for the longest time. But that feels like so long ago, I guess that's what being old is.

The third night I was there, the two of us had dinner and got back to the apartment very late. We talked on the way back about the same old stuff, how work was and all of that. Those are the conversation I prefer having to the one we ended up having.

"I think we need to talk about the way we left things, before I came here." Alice suggested.

"What do you mean by that?" I asked, dancing around answering as much as I could.

"Timmy, you can't make me out to be the bad guy in this situation."

"Who said I made you the bad guy?"

"Please, don't be like that. I know you, I know you do. Cause if you really felt sorry, you would have been the one apologising when I called you not the other way around." We haven't even been together for a week and we're already fighting. Her tone stirred up some untouched rage at the pit of my stomach.

"Ok Alice, sorry. I'm sorry that you left me alone to take care of a kid all by my fucking self. I'm sorry. I'm sorry that you abandoned hope in our entire relationship and left me alone for four fucking years! I'm sorry that you're living a perfectly nice life in Cape Town, while I'm selling watered down vodka to ten year olds so I can buy some fucking bread for my kid...for our kid." It might be wrong, but shouting felt so good. It felt really good.

"Our kid? Oh Jesus Christ Timmy don't act like a hero, and don't you dare act like you were such a bloody saint of a boyfriend. Huh? Is that what you think? Is that what you truly think? That's ridiculous." Her words spat at me like venom, finally I could see her for the snake that she was.

"Of course I wasn't perfect Alice, we were so young when we started dating...people change. I was changing, Alice"

"You were suffocating is what you were." She mumbled under her breath.

"Well, you were a stuck up bitch when you wanted to be." It felt nice to have the final word, and I wanted to leave it like that...so I left.

<u>Odette</u>

I didn't mean to lie, but with the situation going on at home I couldn't imagine introducing my family to Keith. Besides, it's not like we're getting married there really was no reason to meet my parents anyway. I had enough things to worry about myself, I shouldn't be prohibited from being with him just because I was worried of what my parents would say. The thing with Keith and I was, I didn't care how long it lasted and I wasn't concerned with how it was going to end. But of course, I never expected our relationship to change the way it did.

In typical fashion, when I got home there was some sort of commotion with my mother and father. I had never seen them actually fight or anything, they were rather quiet. But I always saw what I gauged as the aftermath of a fight. This time, Mama had her small Ralph Lauren bag clutched firmly in her pale hands as she looked over me. "Odette, I'm going away for a bit alright. I'm going to stay with your aunt. You'll stay here." She was already moving towards the door as she said this and her sharp shoulder sliced past me, they nudged me further into the house while she went further away.

Interestingly enough, I didn't say anything. It wasn't because I was upset or in shock, it was because I was...relieved. I was relieved. If Mama was gone that meant I had much more freedom. I had nobody to check in on me, I could actually be my own person for once in my whole life.

Now, looking back at it I wished Tata went and Mama stayed. If I had the slightest idea of what was going to happen, I would have asked them to swap places. But nobody can be in charge of other people's fate. You can only be in charge of your own.

<u>Alice</u>

Dear Timmy,

Keith was in very bad shape when he arrived. He walked in with you, laughing as he told some story. I heard them from upstairs, I wasn't expecting laughter so I crept quietly down the stairs so as to not disturb you. Keith was skinny with black shaggy hair and a big smile, does he still look like that? He was wearing what appeared to be a woman's blouse that was all the way open with faded jeans. He had purple bruises all over his chest and on his forearms. I greeted him with a hug, suddenly realising why he came home with you. His big warm smile was quite juxtaposing to the blackeye he bared.

"Hi, I'm Keith. Sorry uh, sorry for the trouble." My heart immediately melted. You know when you meet somebody and you can instantly tell that they're very sweet but very troubled? Keith is that type of person.

"I'm Alice. It's no trouble at all sweetheart."

"Well, you guys don't need to make food or anything like that. I'll be leaving you guys alone now," said Keith motioning towards the door.

"Nonsense Keith, where would you stay? You're staying with us from now on ok, that's what that police guy said anyway. Remember the talk we had in his office? Alice is going to go put some things in the guest room, we don't have much but uh...it's enough for us, and for you too." Keith smiled and gave each of us a teary-eyed hug. "Bless you guys," he kept on saying. I've never met a child who was so grown up. A scary amount too, you would have thought he was our age. We sat down on the floor and had a dinner of canned fish and bread. Keith ate fast as if the food would run away, the red sauce staining his blouse.

"Where did you get that blouse, Keith?" I asked because my curiosity was getting the better of me.

"What's a blouse?" I pointed at his blouse. He looked down at it and smiled. "You talk real fancy." He said, half amused. He told me the blouse belonged to his friend's girlfriend, and that she had given it to him. "I had a shirt myself but it's broken now and, well it's coming winter soon so I thought I'll borrow hers until I buy one for myself or those charity people come with donations again."

In the guest room (which was probably intended to be a washing machine room) I laid out a thin roll-out mattress and took a thick blanket off our bed for him. It's always cold at night. He was very grateful about the whole ordeal and said it was his first time getting a bed in a long while. He was quite calm about the whole thing as if his parents didn't just die a brutal death. But in the night-time, I hear him cry in his sleep. Every night that he's been here, but then in the mornings he's calm and quiet.

We fought that night, not properly but I did try and express my feelings to you. I told you that we weren't ready to look after a child and that I was scared. Of course, in retrospect you were in a corner because you didn't ask for Keith, he was simply sprung upon you. But he wasn't my responsibility, although I didn't say it like that when we had this initial argument. Not because I didn't know, but because I wanted to leave everything with you. I wanted both of us to be cut from all ties, and be together without any responsibilities. Nothing holding us back. But then, with the child, it was one other thing weighing us down.

You dismissed me, instead explaining how Keith found his parent's bodies himself and that the only reason he was wearing the woman's blouse was that his clothes were dirty with blood. Naturally, this made me emotional and I abandoned the point of my argument. Reassuring you that we could take care of Keith together, just the two of us. I think we both had the same thought if we had turned him back to the police and said we weren't fit to be his parents if we were to abandon him...wouldn't that make us just as bad as his parents?

Love, Alice

<u>Keith</u>

"And what exactly are you planning on doing with this?" I asked Mickey. Of course, I was not surprised that he gotten a gun, but for the life of me I had no clue what he'd use it for.

"To shoot you, kiddo. I'll shoot your fuckin brains out." He shouted pointing the short, black rusted thing at me. No safety on the thing either...you just needed to pull the trigger.

"Oh I'd kill you first," I joked, trying to grab the gun out of his hands.

"You'd never shoot a gun kid, you're too innocent for that shit. You're the virgin Mary herself kid." He joked, as if he had shot somebody before.

We played around a bit more with the gun, taking turns passing it around and "shooting" each other.

Then BAM, his door flew open and this big buff guy and this little guy were staring us dead in the face. I was just about to ask them if everything was alright but when I looked over at Mickey he was scared senseless, his green eyes shrinking into the back of his head. His gun was in his left hand. He stood up tall, pretending to look all tough but I knew him, and I'd only ever seen him that scared once before.

"Keith, get out ok. Now" He wasn't looking at me, he was looking straight at these two big guys. I was pretty chilled about it at first though, so I walked to the door like Mickey asked but these two big guys were blocking it. Right when I was about to ask them to budge the one guy knocked me right in the eye, and his friend kicked the wind right out of my stomach. I fell back on the ground, my heart pounding in my bloody eye socket. I held my head but it was numb, like pins and needles in my brain. I didn't get into fights, the only person who would beat me like this was my dad, but he wasn't there so I had no reason to be violent anymore. I'd never fight somebody the way I fought him. Never again.

"Hey what the fuck man?" asked Mickey. I was about to look up at him to ask who on earth these guys were, but they answered it for me.

"GIVE US THE DAMN MONEY." The one big guy shouted, my God was Mickey using loan sharks?

"I'll have it by the end of the week I promise ok? I'm getting paid the end of the week ok I promise!"

"How are we supposed to believe that? Why would we believe some junkie like you." Mickey's not a junkie anymore though. So what was he using the money for? Did he relapse? Was I right? No. No there's something else going on. There has to be.

"He's been sober for two years now, Jack." The little guy said. I'll be honest, wasn't expecting him to defend Mickey like that. It kinda defeated the dramatic entrance.

"I know he has, Carl. I was trying to be scary you fuckin twat." The big guy argued, sounding way more offended than he shoulda been.

"You said you'd stop calling me that," the little guy (or "Carl" I guess) whined.

"And you said you weren't sleeping with my girlfriend but look how that turned out."

I'm not a smart guy but I think fast under pressure. Realising, that those two guys were actual idiots and having their own private conversation, I thought I could try help Mickey out. "Here." I mumbled, reaching into my back pocket. I handed the keys to Jack (the big guy). "It's the keys to Mr Rain's Shack. How about you take these and when Mick gives you the money at the end of the week you give us these." Carl and Jack inspect the keys, then Jack shoved it in his pant pockets, leather pants because of course they were leather pants.

Carl looked at Mickey, adjusting his poster to make himself look taller. "Sunday by the docks, we'll meet you there. That black chick of yours. Lotus I think? Yeah, that's her name. The one that works on the other side. I see she's been taking the night shifts. We'll be sure to keep an eye on her, there are some dangerous people around you know. Who knows what could happen to her."

"Wow Carl, threating the safety of his girlfriend, cleaver one Carl." Jack mumbles, rolling his eyes. Then, they kinda just pissed off, just like that. I couldn't imagine that these were the same loan sharks that beat that kid up, they couldn't even threaten properly.

I turned my head to Mickey, watched as the blood boiled under his tan skin, less out of fear and more out of being pissed off. When Mickey said that loan sharks were stupid I didn't think he meant that they were literal idiots like those guys. Well, at that point I was still laying on the ground and Mickey walked over to me and sat down, I couldn't see so great outta my left eye, but he looked like he was about to cry.

"I thought you said that loan sharks are stupid." I didn't know what else to say.

"They are kiddo, they are. I just, I need the money."

"What do you need a loan for anyway?"

"Rent."

"Bullshit. Lotus pays rent." He went quiet.

"Oh god this is bad. This is, this is really bad." He stood up and started pacing around.

"Just tell me Mickey. Come on you can tell me anything, what's going on."

He started talking about this chick he used to date, before Thandi. I didn't really understand why he was talking about her and I didn't remember who this chick was. Mickey's been with a lot of chicks. Then, well then he went onto to say that she got pregnant. Shit.

"Wait, how old were you?"

"Sixteen." Well, that's not super young for a kid I don't think. But I was still kinda shocked, we were supposed to know everything about each other, at least I thought I knew everything about him. Then he tells me that he's got a kid. Mickey's got a kid.

"I'm a little behind on child support and well, if I don't pay up soon I'll get arrested. She had a court order and everything, so if I don't pay up all the money I owe her I'll get arrested because I was supposed to pay her every month but I never did. So I borrowed some money from these guys, and I thought the money from the robbery with that money would be enough but it isn't. But don't worry, ok kiddo? We'll just hit another house, I'll pawn it off before the week ends and then I'll send the money to her and everything will be ok. I'm not going to get arrested."

I didn't want Mickey to go jail, I know what type of stuff happens to people in jail. My dad went to jail and he told me what he had to go through, real disgusting things happened to him. He was different when he came back from jail. I was not going to let that happen to Mickey. I would not let him turn into that. I thought I'd never have to think about that stuff again, but you always end up thinking about what you thought you'd never end up thinking about. Always end up seeing what you never thought you'd see. Always end up doing what you thought you'd never do.

<u>Alice</u>

Dear Timmy,

Keith might be the most interesting child I've ever met. He likes old music and hand-rolled cigarettes, and he likes his mangoes sliced on a piece of bread. He woke up early in the mornings and washed himself with a bucket outside and then he would sit outside the house and watch the sky. He was like an old man and a little kid rolled into one.

I remember his friend, Mickey. You didn't like him that much when you first heard about him. We didn't know plenty about him except for the fact that he was a paid fighter and on drugs. I never questioned his friendship with Keith as I never met him and I felt it wasn't my place to judge who he chose to be friends with. But, you were worried about Mickey's influence on Keith.

At that time, I realised that you must have been fired since you

So because I didn't want to upset you, I talked to Keith. The conversation went a little something like this:

"How was your day?" He shrugged and said that the weather was quite "sticky." I told him that he should say humid next time, the weather was quite humid.

"How's your friend...Mickey?"

"He's ok you know. He's staying at his girlfriend's house so I was there helping him because he's a little sick right now."

"Really, does he have a flu or something?" I asked, suddenly curious.

"Nah, going through withdrawals? I think that's how you say it."

I was surprised by his honesty and relaxed nature. Then Keith went on to say he's seen people behave way worse when they go through withdrawals and that Mickey's simply sleeping now.

"He's just a bit weak that's all, he was vomiting a bit but that's normal. Anyway, I don't wanna talk about that anymore." Then he mumbled something under his breath and started picking at this dried wound he has on the side of his stomach.

"How are you feeling about your parents?" I think it's best to ask him that question once in a while.

Especially since he hasn't been acting like what I would expect a grieving person to act like.

He shrugged. "I think if I don't think too much about it, I feel fine. Sometimes even relaxed."

Strange thing to say, I thought. "Well, do you miss them at all?"

Something about him shifted when I asked that. His face became less animated.

"No, the whole reason they went on that boat was to be away from me, so I think that tells you pretty much everything about them. I don't blame them though, they were getting old anyway."

"You think they were old?" I asked.

"People like us, we're not supposed to live that long."

Lanky

When I was about thirteen, the time I started high school I really wanted to enter poetry in this poetry competition. All my friends thought it was girly and stupid, but I didn't care. I just wanted to enter poetry for this competition. So when I'd get home and my dad was beating my mother to death in the other room I didn't care, I'd go to my safe space in the corner and write this poem for the competition.

I think I was so focused on myself and all the things I wanted to do because it was a distraction. Well, when my parents sent me away to live with my grandmother I didn't care. I didn't care about my mom or my dad or anybody else. I was so damn upset that I was going to miss the poetry competition. So when I got to the island the only thing I was focussed on was myself, and my own distractions. I used to have passion for life when I was young, I used to write I used to have friends I used to be happy. Not all the time, I'm a human after all but man, when I was happy I was really happy.

Something changed when my grandmother died, a switch in my brain a sudden realisation. It was my fault. I know people say that when a loved one dies but I couldn't be more serious. It's a small world. People focus too much on themselves they end up losing people that are close to them. If you're too careful living by yourself everybody else will end up dying. All around you, your life can change in a heartbeat. It's important to know your surroundings, know the people you're with and protect the people you love. I didn't even know my grandmother that well, I had two whole years to get to know her and I wasted them on trying to figure myself out.

Everything in life is a huge chore. School and finding work of course, then even dating Alice wasn't the same. I didn't feel passion or excitement or anything. I didn't feel anything. I operated on autopilot, and I knew deep down she must have been aware. But she didn't say anything so I assumed she was happy. I was doing my job. Ticking another thing off the checklist. Sometimes I think I haven't been conscious in my own body since I was a child. But I don't know if that's a terrible thing...it's safer that way, it's easier.

In some strange way, telling Alice all this seemed like I was explaining something that was already explained. Maybe she had always known it and it was just about me figuring it out on my own. After I walked out of her apartment and finally finished reading those last letters, I kinda understood that maybe there are two sides to the story.

"I wish you had told me at the time, then we wouldn't have had to go through all this shit."

"You know I would have if I thought I could." Alice tilted her head upwards, smiling slightly.

"I'm sorry I didn't listen to you, properly. I'm sorry I didn't read between the lines."

"It's ok, I'm sorry that I was so co-dependant."

"I love you." I think that's something you say after telling your girlfriend that you're a terrible person.

"I love you too." Quiet. It was nice to be quiet in that room for a while, sometimes even without looking at her I know what face she's thinking and it turns out I was thinking the same thing too.

"I should get Keith, and take care of things back there before I come back, shouldn't I?" Nodding her head in agreement, she sat herself down on my lap.

"Don't go just yet, stay for one more day at least." She combed her fingers through my hair.

"Ok, I'll leave tomorrow. " I hesitated.

"It's best to bring him here. He's better off here than there, we all are."

Alice

Dear Timmy,

I know I haven't mentioned the fight we had, and I know we've been talking on the phone about you coming to visit me, but before you come I should explain why I said what I said so that you hopefully don't hold any resentment.

I left sometime in March, a little after my birthday. We hadn't been talking to each other at all, which was fine with me and I honestly thought you didn't care either. I had been very occupied with taking care of Keith and you were occupied with trying to find good work,

Then, on that day that I left, you finally broke the silence.

You asked me if I was ok, using that typical soft voice tactic. I stood up and moved away from you, I was facing you now, why did you look so much older than I remember? How long have we been together, have I aged at the same pace as you?

"You should ask yourself that question."

You scoffed. "What does that mean? Listen, I'm sorry we haven't been able to chill together as much."

"You didn't tell me you got fired." You're silent, so I continue. "You don't say anything to me, and I know you're taking jobs around the harbour, but why can't you just tell me that yourself?"

"I'm sorry that my fucking work ethic is an inconvenience for you."

"I'm not happy anymore, Timmy. We're not happy, we're not happy together anymore. I don't want to be with somebody like you anymore." That was the one honest truth.

I don't know when I started crying but tears were rolling with every word. I was clutching my stomach the pain felt unbearable like I hadn't eaten in years.

"You...you don't want to be with me anymore? So that's it? Is that the reason why you're saying all of this nonsense...because you need some excuse to leave me? You fucking bitch, when have I ever done anything to hurt you?"

You stood up, somehow you looked smaller than I remembered. You were paler too, crouching over himself and moving backwards like some kind of monster.

"I love you. But I can't do this anymore. I'm sorry." I put my hand on your shoulder, you flinched for a second and I swear for a moment I thought you were going to hit me.

You shrugged, completely ignoring what I had to say. "I don't know what you want from me anymore." He replied.

So I finally did it.

I left.

<u>Odette</u>

I met Alex outside her house and we decided to go together. She did online schooling and tended to be quite busy but that day she was free. "Did you hear about the supposed robbery?" She asked, pulling her blonde fringe away from her eyes to reveal her large and pale forehead.

"No...what robbery?"

"Well apparently that old house that belongs to Mr and Mrs Green was robbed. There's no sign of forced entry but somebody saw some people climb out of the window and run to the beach."

"So why don't the police do anything?" I asked.

Alex sighed. "I don't know, the police here are kind of shit."

In all honesty, I was barley listening to Alice tell me things that had nothing to do with me. Robberies were so far away from my world and something I could never imagine being involved in in any sort of way. What I was really thinking about was myself, and what I was going to do with my life since Mama left. I thought I would like it better with her gone. But it was worse than I thought, maybe I was used to having her tell me what to do and doing what she said but now without that I felt confused. It was like always being in a crowded room your whole life and then suddenly left isolated and on your own. With your own jumbled up thoughts to ponder on. I thought that's what I wanted, the freedom. But it didn't feel good, it felt unsettling. Like I was moving in limbo through a liminal space.

<u>Keith</u>

I don't like to think about the night my parents left. I don't like to think about a lot of things but the night my parents left was the worst night of my life. It's not because I found them dead a couple days later, because honestly I don't care about that. It was bound to happen eventually. But that night, that night I saw a version of myself that I don't want to see again. I wouldn't ever bring myself back to that person again.

We left to our second robbery at ten, me and Mickey had told Skippy and Thandi about the urgency of our plan and they both seemed pretty chilled with the idea of another robbery. We had got about two hundred each from the first one which is a lot for us but it was not enough for Mickey to be safe. The house was close to the museum...which was close to the police station. Seemed a little counterproductive but Skippy said that life was nothing but a "get rich or die trying" situation. I think he got that from a movie but whatever. Mickey was more quiet than usual, had this regretful look in his eyes which was fuckin scary. I don't think Mickey's ever regretted anything in his life before. I guess there are more things he kept to himself than I thought. Well, anyway we felt pretty prepared going into the house and we had our usual black plastic bag and torch situation.

We shoved Skippy in a small crack by the window and heard something kinda loud drop.

"Fuck was that?" Mickey asked looking over Thandi and me.

"Sorry, that was the gun, it's ok though. Come, let's get you guys in here." Skippy whisper-shouted, opening the window from inside. The white paint was chipping off.

"My gun?" Mickey half yelled. Skippy was such an idiot, nobody asked him to bring the gun. Nobody asked Skippy to do anything except shut up once in a damn while.

"Let's not argue ok? Keith will keep the gun with him. Nobody's gonna shoot the damn thing," Thandi reasoned with Mickey which seemed to calm him down.

One by one we crawled through the window which turned out to be a bathroom. The bathroom was empty, besides a bath and sink which we couldn't really steal. I had never used an actual bath before, maybe I should have taken it. But I guessed, if we did enough of those jobs I could buy myself a bathroom just like that one.

But as we looked around in the house, we didn't find shit. Absolutely nothing, most people leave some stuff around even if they don't stay on the island full time but that place was empty, would have thought a corpse was in the other room, the way it was so dead.

"Now what?" Skippy asks, looking over at Mickey and Thandi. I would have liked to make another two hundred to put away for myself. But most importantly, Mickey could have gotten into something serious. We needed the money, like right that instant.

"Christ, I don't know. Shit! What are we gonna do?" Mickey shouted, surely making a noise. He crouched down with his head in his hands absolutely freaking out.

"Wait! Come on guys there's one other place I know."

Odette told me that her parents left on business and that she was staying with Alice in the meantime. When I saw her yesterday with Alice they said so, so If we went to take a couple stuff from Odette's everything would be fine. Besides, her parents are so rich I doubt they would even notice. We'll make sure not to take anything from her bedroom. I explained my plan to Mickey on the way and he was half impressed, half concerned.

"Trust me, ok? I trust you all the time." This was reassuring enough for Mickey.

So, we were walking down the path that Mickey and I took for delivery and it was pitch black. Nobody was out and most of the house lights were off. The silence was relaxing, the sound of the ocean was always in the background but it felt louder. Like white noise. I wondered what life would be like outside of the island, soon enough I'd know.

No chance that the front door would be open, so instead we wrapped around the house and entered in the storage room at the back. Filled with cardboard boxes and one dim light giving off this almost sickly yellow glow. I really liked Odette but I'd always found certain things about her house to be real creepy.

"Who leaves their storage room unlocked?" Skippy asked as he peered into the different boxes.

"I don't fucking know, come on let's go into the main house." Thandi hadn't spoken a word, as though she wasn't too sure about this idea. She preferred for things to be planned out properly.

The white marble of the house was creepy, and I felt like the tiles were gonna look over at us and say "hey, you don't belong here." It felt like there were eyes everywhere even though the house was completely empty. Everything was so clean, so our movements become more careful and delicate than usual. Mickey and Thandi moved to the kitchen and living room, carefully inspecting different items for them to take. I took Skip with me up the crystal clear stairs. I felt like we were making the house dirtier just by breathing. There was no noise, I couldn't hear the ocean or Skippy or anything. I could only hear my own heart beating right in my face.

"Go right I'll go left." I told Skippy and he disappeared down the corridor while I walked the other way. There was a painting hanging on the wall, it was a mountain or maybe a rock or something it was very unclear. The more I stared, the more uncomfortable I got. I walked further down, it was dark but there was some moonlight coming in from a hole in the roof covered by glass. The sky was clear, the stars weren't around. The further down I walked the more deaf I felt, I couldn't hear anything except for my own crooked footsteps.

My feet stopped me because there's a door. I didn't even notice it before because it blended in with the white wall, except for the silver handle. Was it a bedroom door? Maybe it was Odette's room, I'd feel creepy going into her room without asking her. But I opened the door anyway, the handle was so cold it stung the palm of my hand. It was one of those bedrooms that was like its own house. Bookcase and some sort of golden swan decoration. I touched it...real gold... definitely real. I grabbed it, surely the golden swan could be the key to helping Mickey out. Curious of what else I could find I walked further down, right round a corner.

Stop. There's a big kind sized bed. Stop. Is somebody sleeping in it? Yes! There's definitely somebody in that bed, far too big to be Odette. Is it her father, but she said they weren't home. Why would she lie about that? I move closer until I'm staring right at his face. He's definitely asleep, he looks peaceful there in his sleep, in his big white bed, in a big white house in a big white neighbourhood. And suddenly all the sound comes rushing back into my head, the water, the sand and his breathing. He's breathing so peacefully. Huh, I reckon rich people sleep the best.

Shit! He's going to wake up I can just feel it. We need to get out right now before he calls the police or I don't know, Christ I'm like ten centimetres away from his face. If I move he'll hear me, and I'm holding a gun in my left hand with the golden swan in my right. I slowly retract my head away from this guy and sigh because I think I can get away without him realising. But then....his eyes snap open and he jumps back right out of his bed. He's tall, a big tall guy who's of course wearing white.

"Who are you?" His eyes damn near bulging out of his face, I feel the tips of my ears flash red I'm scared senseless right now. But then I remember, he knows me! Odette said she told him about me, sure it's a weird way to meet me but at least I have a chance. But why would she lie about him being here? Did he come early, is he sick? Is her mother also in the house? What if one of the others bumped into her the way I did now? Would I even be able to hear them call for me or hear her scream?

"I'm Keith, Odette's boyfriend." My hands are behind my back so he can't see the gun or the swan. At that point, I was more worried about him seeing the swan than the gun.

His face shrinks and his eyes retract as they do an up and down movement. He's inspecting me. Then he winces at me in disgust. Why was he doing that? I'm not a bad person why is he looking at me like that? Why is his expression hurting me so much, why can't I breathe anymore?

"What are you talking about, my daughter has no boyfriend and certainly not you. How would you even know her name? I'm going to have to call the police immediately young man."

No. No he can't do that, I can't put Mickey and them in danger like that. I can't put myself in danger like that. My clammy and shaky hand raises and I hold the gun at his face. His hands instinctively raise up and suddenly he's scared. He's scared of me, he's disgusted yes but he's scared. He gets down on his knees and his eyes are pleading. How strange...I have the power now. Is power the same as fear? Why is he so scared, yet even in his fear I can see the disapproval written all over his face.

I'm not violent, I'm not a violent person but my hand is on the trigger. He didn't even look like himself, no...he looked like her.

"I only hit him because he was hurting you, mom! That's the only reason." But there's no response only silence.

"Please stop looking at me like that, why does everyone always look at me like that?!"

But she's not responding...she's dead. She's dead because I drove them away...she's dead because she hates me. She's dead because she's disgusted in me. I thought I wasn't like that but maybe this is me. Maybe this is who I am.

So I shoot him. BANG. I shoot him because I can. BANG. I shoot him because she lied. BANG. They all lie, all the time. I shoot because I'm angry. BANG. I shoot because I am my father's son and maybe there's nothing I can do to change it. BANG. This is me, this is who I am. BANG. I'm not who I want to be, nobody else is who I want them to be, and it's not my fault...so I shoot. BANG. BANG. BANG.

There was blood all over the window, there was blood on the roof. There was blood on the doors and in my mouth and I'm crying. I wanted to walk up to him and say that I was sorry because I thought he was somebody else but there was so much blood everywhere I was gonna be sick. He was still looking at me. Was he dead did I kill him? What happened to his face why was a piece of it missing? Why was there so much blood in his room? Since when were the walls red?

I turned around and Skippy, Thandi and Mickey were looking at me. Thandi's hands were covering her mouth and Skippy was crying. But Mickey was just staring straight at me. So I put the gun in my pocket and I wiped the blood splatter from my forehead and Mickey mumbled. "Keith?" Like he can't recognise me or maybe I was too far away because I felt so tall in that room. "It's ok Mickey. I feel better now."

<u>Odette</u>

That evening Alex and I had spent in her room getting drunk off vodka from her parents' drinks cabinet until it ran out. Which seemed to make me feel a little better, at least for a little bit.

"Hey why don't we go over to my house I think there's more drinks there." I suggested, assuming that my father was asleep in his bed and knowing that he wouldn't bother us regardless.

We walked in the dead of night through the neighbourhood to my house. Surprisingly, our neighbours had their lights turned on even though it was late especially considering the age of most of the people who lived around there, they usually went to bed quite early.

"Is there some old person funeral that we don't know about?" Alex joked as we stumbled to the front door and I rummaged in my pocket for the keys, carefully opening the door. Part of me never wanted to see that house ever again and now even more so.

"Alex, how about you go to the kitchen, the drinks are there. I'm just gonna go upstairs to see if Tata is awake."

I said, walking up the stairs but something felt wrong. At the time, I assumed it was because I was tipsy and my friend was currently stealing alcohol from the kitchen but there was an unexplainable feeling of dread clasping its claws around my frail shoulders. There was a long corridor upstairs, the right went to my bedroom and the left went to Tata and Mama's room. Motioning to the right I was abruptly stopped by the sound of mumbling coming from my room.

"Hello?" Was is Tata? No, what would he be doing in there? More mumbling and then the sound of my window cracking open. I sprinted to my room, a pale figure slipped right out of my bedroom window. I looked down from the window, a white boy with light hair scurrying down the street slipped away into the darkness. Alex must have heard me calling because when I turned my head she was there.

"What the hell was that?" She asked, with a puzzled expression as she peered over my shoulder.

"I wonder if Tata saw anything, I think he's still asleep. I mean, I barely saw that boy."

I walked down the corridor to his room, calling out "Tata? Tata it's me!" A very distinct and unusual metallic smell wafted in the air. I moved faster, his door was open I walked inside gingerly, walked into his cold room.

Blood everywhere, on the walls, on the bed all over the floor and bloody footsteps. I couldn't breathe, my heart wasn't beating anymore everything was still. "Oh God! Shit I need to call the police right now." Alex shouted, but I couldn't turn to her.

"Tata!" This was more of a scream than a call, less of a question. Moving closer and closer, around the bend of the bed. There he was. There Tata was. Eye's open, blood pooling at his hands. A hole where the right half of his face should be, chunks of meat on the floor next to him. Bullet casings everywhere. What monster would do something like this? And yet, even in my pain and intense shock I did not go up to him. I inched back, with my hand over my mouth. He's gone. My father is gone. My father is dead. Was it some sort of sick act from God? I've never been one to believe in him but what a biblical ending to everything. I was relieved, relieved and disgusted in myself for feeling this way. I had to run from him, couldn't be in that room or that house or even on that side of the island. I left Alex on the phone crying to the police, I ran out of that house and I didn't turn back.

My skinny and frail legs carried me all the way to Mickey's house. I opened the door seeing that the lights were still on.

There they were, Keith and Mickey. Keith was drenched in blood, looking down at his shaky hands mumbling to himself. "No. No. No." Mickey was holding him still as if reassuring him that everything was ok. Why was Keith covered in blood what was he doing? I stumbled backward and fell to the ground. This noise made Mickeys head snap in my direction and his eyes grew wider than I'd ever seen them. Keith was still staring at his shaky hands as though he wasn't real. Mickey moved closer to me and I tried crawl backwards, too weak and scared to stand. "GET AWAY FROM ME!" I screamed and hot tears start pouring from my eyes.

"Listen Odette, ok? Please don't make a noise." Mickey tried to reason, as cool as ever but there was this guilty look behind his green eyes. Keith then turns around at this and seeing me, he smiles blood all over his face. He smiles at me as though it's any ordinary day.

"Murderer! Killer! GET AWAY FROM ME THE BOTH OF YOU." I couldn't comprehend what had happened, I had brought myself to them looking for Keith to comfort me and there he was drenched in my father's blood. I got sick on the floor, partly from alcohol and partly because the smell of blood felt so rich in the air. I stood up, took one last look at Keith and left. I vowed to myself that I would never see him again, and that I would never set foot on this island ever again.

....

Would I have behaved differently that night if my present self went back to my teenage self and spoke to her? I think I would have thanked him. I would have said thank you for taking him away. Sometimes, you need a drastic event to realise what's wrong with your life, and understand what's truly important. I guess that's a messed up thing to say, but I've learnt to speak my truth now. I'm not scared anymore. There's nobody left to be scared of.

<u>Keith</u>

I didn't know what was happening, how I got to Mickey's house and what the fuck he was saying to me. The blood was sticky and drying on my hands and all I could do was stare at them. I think Odette came by, but I think we scared her away. I hoped she was ok, I hoped she could understand what happened. Why do people always leave me? Mom, Alice and now Odette. Why would they leave me? Maybe that's the way things are supposed to be, maybe everybody leaves everybody in the end.

"What the fuck is going on?" Lanky steps into the room and shuts the door behind him. Why was he back early? Maybe I was imagining him, for all I knew he wasn't here at all.

"Are you real?" I ask...looking over at his light eyes. He didn't respond instead he walked over to Mickey and spoke to him like I was not there at all.

"What the hell did you do?" Mickey looked so small next to Lanky, his posture was real bad for some reason. Or maybe he was always that small and I hadn't noticed. His eyes were red with tears and he was shaking. Moving around frantically.

"Keith come take off your clothes, go to the bathroom." But Lanky demanded an answer so Mickey gave some half-baked one while he took off my clothes for me because my hands were not moving properly. He said things about breaking into Odette's house, stealing stuff, Skippy and Thandi, Odette's Dad and other things I couldn't understand.

"Keith, is this true?" Lanky was crying now, everybody was crying even Mickey. I was standing in the room with just my underwear not feeling anything at all.

"As you can fuckin see, he's not going to respond right now!" Mickey shouts, taking off his clothes and putting my bloody ones on himself.

While this was happening Lanky was putting Mickey's clothes on me which fit the same.

Lanky pushed me to the bathroom and turned the water in the sink on. The tap water was very dirty there but Lanky used it to wash my face and hands. Talking the whole time, telling me that everything was going to be all right and that him and Mickey would sort things out but I could see the tears in his eyes and I could feel that his hands were shaking and I wanted to say something but I didn't know how.

"I'm so sorry kid. It's my fault that you did this." He cried into my shoulder and I pushed him away because it isn't his fault at all its Mickey's. So I storm into the room where Mickey is crouched down crying harder than I'd ever seen anyone cry. Holding his chest and bawling his eyes out.

"This is all your fault Mickey. You're supposed to protect me you're supposed to be my older brother and you failed." I didn't know where the words are coming from. He looked at me, red in the face and he nods his head.

"I'm a killer because of you! We broke into that house because of you! He's dead because of you! The only reason I did this is because I wanted to help you! The only reason I'm in this mess is because I listened to you! You're a terrible brother, I hate you! I fucking hate you! You've ruined my fucking life! "

Mickey was crying and apologising and Lanky was telling us to keep it down.

"Listen kid, I've got the gun ok? I'm going to go over to the police and tell them I did it. Lanky is gonna take you off the island ok kiddo?"

I didn't respond because I didn't know what to say. Lanky has his hand over his mouth and his pupils were so small in his face like he was looking at ghost, but he was just looking at Mickey.

"I'm sorry I've been a shit brother ok kid? I love you, I know you know that but I'm telling you in case you forgot. I love you. Tell Lotus I love her too, tell her she deserves better." He's walking to the door.

"They're gonna arrest you, Mickey. They'll put you away for life." Lanky shouted, grabbing onto my arm. I don't know why he told him that because he already knew, we all knew.

Mickey turned around and I saw that smile of his again, and I knew that was the last time I'd see that smile. "It's ok you guys, it was gonna happen one way or another." Then, he's gone.

While we were walking I tried not to think about what I did. I tried but it didn't work anymore. I had opened the floodgates and everything was rushing out. There were so many things I wanted to say, to so many people...but I didn't know how. I'm scared I'll feel like this forever. I'm scared.

Lanky didn't say a single thing on our way to the harbour. We sat on the bench and he didn't say anything. He goes to the booth to get our tickets out of here but he didn't say nothing. We left and he didn't say anything, we got on the boat in complete silence. I didn't feel happy or sad or some complicated emotion I don't understand. I only felt numb. Lanky wrapped his arms around me like I was going to run away, like he was protecting me...but everything's already happened.

There's nothing left to protect me from.